D1055700

Look Both Ways
in the Barrio Blanco

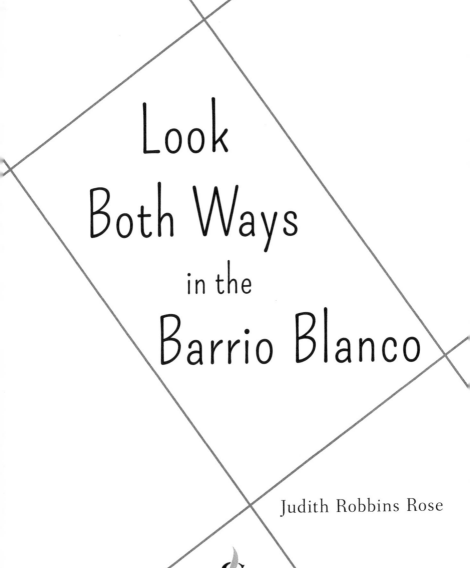

Look
Both Ways
in the
Barrio Blanco

Judith Robbins Rose

CANDLEWICK PRESS

First edition 2015

Library of Congress Catalog Card Number 2014944903
ISBN 978-0-7636-7235-5

BVG 20 19 18 17 16 15
10 9 8 7 6 5 4 3 2 1

Printed in Berryville, VA, U.S.A.

This book was typeset in Fairfield LH.

Candlewick Press
99 Dover Street
Somerville, Massachusetts 02144

visit us at www.candlewick.com

Para "mis hijas,"
Rubi, Perla y Esmeralda;
para la madre de las niñas

———

And for my sons,
Forrest and August

1

WHEN MRS. ESPINOSA announced that 5News was coming to the Maplewood Youth Rescue Center, we all cheered, but me the most. I love movies, and television is kinda like movies, although I didn't watch American TV. And I never watched the news.

But this was my chance to meet somebody famous.

On the day 5News was supposed to come, I was late getting to the youth center. I'd left Mamá's sweater in my locker at school and had to run back for it. Angélica didn't wait like she'd promised. So when I saw her jumping up and down with the other girls in front of the youth center, I darted across the parking lot to tell her off.

Tires squealed, and I jumped. The guy driving the 5News truck had slammed on the brakes. He had to, or he'd have run me over.

If I'd known how the afternoon would turn out, maybe I would've let him.

The TV lady in the seat next to him was fixing her makeup when she was thrown toward the dashboard. She flopped back into her seat, her mouth hanging open and her eyes bulging out. A trail of lipstick zigzagged across her cheek.

I'd never seen anybody famous in real life. She looked *disheveled,* with her sunglasses sliding down her nose and her hair standing up all weird.

But mostly she looked like herself. Like her ginormous picture on Broadway, where her toothy smile stretched five feet across the billboard.

I looked at Angélica and the other girls, and giggled. That's called *nervous laughter.*

The driver climbed out of the truck, carrying a TV camera. Me and about a million other kids from the youth center bounced around, shouting for him to take our picture. We chased him inside the building, forgetting all about the lady with lipstick on her face.

By the time she'd fixed it and walked into the art room, the camera guy was taking videos of us while we made picture frames for Mother's Day.

Mrs. Espinosa and the other women at the youth center buzzed around the TV lady like a swarm of bees. *Do you need anything? A cup of coffee, perhaps?*

She flashed a smile with lots of teeth in it. "Cream and sweetener, please."

Two women ran to get it.

My best friend, Angélica, never glanced up. But I couldn't stop looking at the TV lady. Her sweater matched her eyes — blue and sparkly — and her hair was the color of a new penny.

She noticed me and smiled. The kind of smile I'd see on Mamá's face when she knew I was up to something. Then I remembered I'd jumped in front of the lady's news truck.

"So, you were in a hurry?" she asked.

I swallowed. "I wanted to meet you, Miss."

She raised an eyebrow. "You could've ended up as the lead story."

Now—more than a year later—I know that the *lead story* is the most important news, so it comes first in the show. Miss was saying I could get squished running out in traffic. Grown-ups always tell you to look both ways for cars when crossing the street. But nobody tells you to watch out for the people who cross your path.

My face got hot, and I dragged my eyes away. They fell on the picture frame I was painting. The colors at the youth center were wrong, so I mixed mine myself. Just the right shades of pink and purple. Hope and sorrow. Colors that showed what my heart needed to say.

Perfect! My secret plan would work.

I turned to Angélica, who was concentrating on *her* Mother's Day present. "What do you think?"

Angélica studied my frame, then looked back at her own. She wrinkled her nose and shrugged.

She's jealous? I grinned.

Holding up her cell phone, Mrs. Espinosa asked

the TV lady, "Can I get a shot of you with some of the girls?"

The TV lady whipped out a chair and sat between me and Angélica, but my best friend scooted her chair away. I should've done that, too. When your family has a secret, you need to be careful. But I didn't think about it when the camera was pointing at me. I smiled so big that my face hurt.

Flash!

"Do you like art?" asked the TV lady through her teeth.

Flash!

I nodded, then leaned back so she could see my frame.

"Very pretty," she said, not looking at it. Still showing her teeth to the camera, she tilted her head so our hair touched.

Another flash blinded me.

Our photo would be splashed across the next newsletter, along with the headline "Local Celebrity Combats Teen Pregnancy."

Except, I wasn't a pregnant teen. I wouldn't be

twelve for two months, and I didn't even have a boy-friend. But Angélica and the other kids at middle school snickered, asking when my baby was due.

That feeling is called *humiliated.*

Because of the flash, I couldn't see the flowers I'd painted on my frame. Spots floated in front of my eyes.

The stranger stopped showing her teeth. I realized that smiling was part of her job and she got tired of it. Like doing push-ups with your face. Then she really looked at my frame. "I love your colors!"

She noticed! Nobody had admired my artwork since Mamá left. My throat hurt. Like I might cry.

I looked away and saw my older sister, Rosa, sit-ting with the other eighth-graders, frowning. She usually ignored me when her friends were around, but her eyes traveled from me to the TV lady.

Rosa's worried? She thinks I'll say something stupid?

But now I think Rosa was jealous. She wanted to steal Miss from me, even before Miss was really mine.

6

The flock of women came back to flit around her. They presented her with a cup of coffee. A stir stick. A scratchy paper towel from the center's bathroom.

The TV lady bobbed her head at them. "Thank you—I'm sure it's fine—no, really—I just need a minute." She turned back to me. "So, this frame is for your mom?"

The women flapped away, their feathers ruffled because somebody famous would rather talk to a kid. There's a word to describe how I felt.

Flattered.

I nodded. Seeing my photo in the frame would remind Mamá of her promise. I didn't need a picture of her. She was there, every time I closed my eyes. Like her image was tattooed on the inside of my eyelids. "But I still have to glue my name on it."

Wooden letters, painted pink, were lined up on the newspapers protecting the table.

Even without my name on it, Mamá would know I made that frame. She'd see those colors and say, "This is from my Jacinta!" If I hadn't tried to put my name on it, Mamá would've gotten my present.

The camera guy shoved a microphone at the TV lady. "Kate! They're coming to us early!"

"In the A block?" She pushed something into her ear and pulled her sweater to straighten it. Another bright light hit my eyes.

The guy counted, "In three . . . two . . ."

I heard a tinny voice — a man's voice — coming from the thing in the TV lady's ear. She nodded into the light. A tiny red bulb on the camera glowed. *I'm on television?* I prayed that people watching TV couldn't hear my heart pounding.

The lady spoke into the microphone. "That's right, Steve. We're in Maplewood all this week, looking at one community's efforts to integrate its immigrant population. This city is hailed as a model for local governments."

Miss's TV voice was bigger somehow, but not louder. The word for that is *authoritative.* "Today we'll explore how the youth rescue center works to prevent teen pregnancy by offering social support and activities for neighborhood girls."

She stopped talking, her concerned look frozen on her face. The voice in her ear said, "Take video."

The little red light on the camera winked out, and her smile dissolved.

I didn't understand what a bunch of girls making Mother's Day presents had to do with teen pregnancy. But people at the youth center were always *lecturing* us about boys. We'd nod and wait until they got to the fun stuff.

"When we come back live, can we talk a little bit?" she asked me.

"I get to talk on television?"

She smiled. Not the fake TV smile. A smile that climbed up one side of her face. A smile that looked like it belonged there. "That's right."

I smiled, too. "Can I keep working? I need to finish this."

"You're Jacinta?" she asked, reading my name from the wooden letters on the table. She pronounced my name with a *j* sound, like Americans do.

"Ha-cinta. Like an *h*."

"Jacinta?" she repeated. I nodded. "Fine. Keep working on your frame while I ask a few questions."

The camera guy said, "Heads up. Here we come. In three . . . two . . ."

The little red light blinked back on. The TV lady gave the big-teeth smile to the camera. "Steve, one of the center's offerings includes Teen Promise, a club for girls. This afternoon, participants are creating Mother's Day gifts."

So I grabbed the glue bottle, turned it over, and squeezed.

Nothing.

The lady kept talking. "With me is Jacinta. What grade are you in?"

She tilted the microphone at me.

I whispered, "Miss, the glue won't come out."

She smiled wider. "Why don't we do that later? How old are you?"

"But Miss! I have to finish *today.* Can you try it? *Please?*" I pushed the glue bottle at her.

Her eyes flicked over to the camera as she spoke into the microphone. "The girls here have opportunities to work with adult role models. . . ."

She took the glue bottle and squeezed.

Nothing.

Her smile slid off her face. Her eyebrows bunched together as she shook the bottle, then squeezed again.

Glue splurted.

All over my picture frame.

"No!" I shrieked. Pink and purple flowers floated to the top of the spreading white blobs. We both grabbed for the frame, but she tipped her coffee cup. Brown liquid splashed across the newspapers.

I yelped.

"As you can see, we're having technical difficulties," she joked. Shoving the microphone under her arm, she snatched up the scratchy paper towel to wipe off the glue, but the rough brown paper clung to the gummy mess. "Don't worry—we'll fix it."

She sounded stressed *and* calm as she picked at the shreds of paper towel. Her fingernails turned pinkish purple. The frame was scratched, the flowers smeared, with bits of paper sticking out.

The TV lady flipped it over. "It doesn't look *too* bad."

I tried to yank it back, but she was still examining it and didn't let go.

The frame cracked.

We each stared at our own broken piece. We looked at each other. Then we remembered the TV camera.

She pasted her smile back on. "Looks like we've got our work cut out for us. This is Kathryn Dawson Dahl for 5*News First Look.*"

We stared into the light — painful grins stretched across our faces — for the world's longest moment. Then the tiny red light went dark.

"Clear," said the camera guy.

She slapped a hand against her forehead. "Oh, *God!*"

The camera guy said, "I thought this was supposed to be about teen pregnancy?"

I didn't care about their dumb news story. I stared at the broken frame in front of me. It was stupid, but I looked to Angélica for sympathy. She *was* my best friend. For one second I saw surprise. The next moment I saw something else. The word for that look is *satisfaction*. I shoved myself away from the table, ran into the art-supply closet, and slammed the door.

Maybe I was making a big deal out of a stupid picture frame. But it was part of my secret plan to get Mamá back. *I'll put my photo in it. She'll see how much I've grown. She'll feel guilty and come home.* Maybe my plan sounds dumb if you say it out loud, but I had hoped it would work.

If I was being honest, I would've admitted that I was scared Mamá might not get home at all. Papi's cousin never came back. Now I imagine his bones propped against a rock in the desert, his skull grinning a warning to others. But I couldn't think about that. I lived with fear by looking away.

I sank to the floor. The tears burned, ready to come. The tiles in the art-supply closet were cool underneath me.

Perfect for crying.

So when the door opened, I started to tell Mrs. Espinosa that I wasn't coming out.

It wasn't Mrs. E.

It was the lady who ruined my frame, with her face all blotchy. "I'm so sorry."

Mamá always said, "Be polite to white people, because you don't know what they'll do." Families could be ripped apart because someone made an American angry.

"Can you close the door, Miss?"

I said it *politely*.

You'd think a grown-up would know to close the door and let me cry. But she came *into* the closet, *then* closed the door. Even wearing a skinny skirt, she sat down on the floor, right next to me. In the dark.

"I'm sorry about your frame," she repeated.

Part of me wanted to be nice about it. That's called *gracious*. Grace is something it's taken me a long time to understand. But I didn't feel gracious. I felt *bitter*.

"'S okay," I mumbled. Even though it wasn't. I just wanted her to go. My tears wouldn't wait.

"No. It's not okay. I'm obligated, aren't I?"

I blinked, then shrugged. *Maybe* obligated *means*

a clumsy person who breaks stuff? I tried to take a breath, but it came out like a sob.

She pulled me into her arms. "Tell me about it."

My heart slid up into my throat. Even white kids who don't have to be afraid know not to talk to strangers. But her hair spray smelled like flowers. Like Mamá. Her sweater reminded me of Abuelita's afghan. Mamá gave the afghan to me when she left so I'd feel safe. In the dark I could pretend this stranger *was* Mamá.

So I cried. Like a two-year-old. Like my little sister, Suelita.

When was the last time someone held me?

It made me feel real. Since Mamá had left, I'd been a head floating around with no body. I started talking. The lady listened—like Mamá would've—and that made me feel real, too.

I didn't tell everything. I didn't tell how Mamá let me do things when Papi said no. Like the time she took me to the health clinic for a physical so I could go on the sixth-grade camping trip.

And I didn't tell how—before Suelita was

born—I'd leave Rosa in our bedroom and sneak under the covers with Mamá while Papi was at his night job. That was our secret.

Instead I said that Mamá understood about being the middle child because she had four brothers.

I told how kids at school had laughed when I cut my hair so I'd look like a movie star. Mamá had paid a lot of money at the hair place to fix it, not waiting for it to grow out like Papi said.

"But Mamá's forgotten me."

The lady squeezed me. Like a *reflex*. And that made me cry harder. My nose leaked. I leaned in to wipe it on her sweater, but Miss must've thought I wanted to snuggle, because she squeezed me again. "She can't forget you, Jacinta. She'll never forget."

For one second I wanted to rest against her, to let myself melt into her.

But the closet door swung open.

The camera guy. "Kate, I've got the van packed. We'd better go. Maury's really pissed."

The TV lady stood up, dumping me on the floor. A shiny blue bead from her sweater bounced on the tiles in front of me. I picked it up. It glittered in my hand.

She brushed at the wrinkles in her skirt, smearing it with drying pink and purple paint. "Maury can stick it in his ear. Sending me on a live shot after twenty-five years? You think I *like* making a fool of myself?"

"Miss, you dropped this."

She glanced at me, her face angry. But her frown dissolved when she saw me holding the sparkling bead. She made the fake news-lady smile. "Just— throw it away."

But I stuck the bead in my pocket. I found it there yesterday as I packed my old clothes away for Suelita to wear when she's big. That bead is one of the few things I have left. I'm keeping it to remember what I've gained—things like my *vocabulary*— and how much those things have cost me.

The TV lady stalked out the door and down the corridor, her high heels clicking on the tiles.

The camera guy followed her.

Sighing, I went to get Mamá's sweater. I'd been wearing it since she left. It was grubby, especially around the wrists. I wouldn't wash it because it smelled like Mamá. The sweater hung on the back of my chair, but I didn't see it, because there—right there—on the table was the sticky mess that had been my picture frame.

My legs were stiff as I backed away. I couldn't breathe. Pushing past Rosa, I ran down the hall. I flung myself against the heavy front door and bumped into the TV lady, who was standing on the pavement talking to the camera guy.

The lady who ruined my plan to get Mamá back.

I bounced off her and ran.

"Jacinta!" Her voice chased me down the sidewalk.

I heard my name a second time. My sister's voice. The tears I'd held back broke free again. Rosa caught up with me. "You let that lady put you on *television?*"

Little bumps jumped out on my arms. "Don't tell Papi."

"You're crying because of a broken picture frame?"

I swallowed my sobs, still walking. I didn't care

about the stupid frame. I wanted Mamá back. And sometimes—when you're alone in the world—you want someone to blame.

Like a pushy stranger.

Why would I want such a person in my life?

That's a really good question.

SINCE I'D LEFT Mamá's sweater at the youth center, I missed having it the next day at school. Like I was naked on the playground.

Worse than naked.

I wasn't safe.

So after school when Rosa ordered me to get Suelita from Tía's apartment, I said no.

Rosa said, "You have to. Papi says I'm in charge until Mamá comes home."

"You're not the boss of me." I turned and walked toward the youth center, leaving her to shout at my back. I stuck my fingers in my ears, yelling over my shoulder, "La-la-la-la-la-la! I can't hear you!"

Maybe if I'd gotten to the youth center one minute later, my life would be different. If I'd had to tie my shoelace. If the light had said DON'T WALK when I got to the corner. Miss might've left the package at the front counter for me and forgotten all about being *obligated*.

That's not what happened.

After I grabbed my sweater off the back of the chair in the art room, I almost bumped into Miss again, just outside. With sunglasses hiding her sparkly eyes and a scarf covering her copper hair, you might think I wouldn't recognize her. She looked like a movie star hiding from photographers.

So I knew it was Miss.

"Hello again!" She smiled, wide and white, like in a toothpaste commercial. As if I should be happy to see her.

And it was weird, because I was.

"Here." She handed me a pink paper bag. "For your mom."

Why does she have a gift for Mamá?

There's a word for how I felt. *Wary.* Kids aren't supposed to take gifts from strangers. I thought about saying "No, thank you" and walking away.

But then I'd never know what was in the bag.

It was a silver picture frame. Cut in fancy letters across the bottom was one word.

JACINTA

If I'd been a cartoon, my eyes would've popped out. *When Mamá sees my photo in this, she'll come home!*

I was going to say thank you, but my mouth started moving before the right words could get there. "Miss, will you be my Amiga?"

Amiga means "friend" in Spanish, but at the youth center, it meant a lady to take you places. Not every girl had one. There were never enough volunteers.

The girls with Amigas argued about whose was best. The rest of us pretended we didn't want one. We said only braggers had Amigas.

Angélica talked about her Amiga's *Mercedes* — a car rich people drive. The rest of us listened while the green monster grew in our bellies. Having an Amiga was like finding treasure. Better, because treasure gets spent, and people stay with you.

I never asked myself if two people as different as Miss and me could ever really be *amigas*.

Miss smiled. "Sure!"

Mrs. Espinosa burst out of the youth center. "Kathryn! I'm rushing to an appointment, but I could make a little time if—"

Miss said, "No, no. I'm here for Jacinta. And— call me Kate."

"She's going to be my Amiga!" I blurted.

Mrs. Espinosa beamed at Miss. "Great! I'll get you an application!"

The smile slid off Miss's face. "Application?"

Mrs. E.'s eyes flicked over to me, then back to Miss. "The Amiga program is a mentorship."

Miss turned red. Red like a stoplight, and just as fast. "Mentor? I just thought—" Miss glanced at me, then turned back to Mrs. E. "What—exactly— are we talking about?"

"It's a one-year commitment—" Mrs. E. started.

"Oh. No. Sorry."

I looked down so Miss wouldn't see my tears. Angélica was always calling me Leaky Lids.

Then Miss said, "I brought a little something

to make it right with Jacinta for ruining her picture frame yesterday, but I seem to be making it worse."

"Let me see," said Mrs. E., eyeing the bag I was holding.

Hands shaking, I showed her the frame.

"It has my name on it!" I begged, using what Rosa calls my puppy-dog eyes.

Mrs. E. ignored my eyes. Instead she gave Miss a pained look. "Kate, we don't give expensive gifts to the kids. It causes problems."

Then Mrs. Espinosa looked at me. "And you should know better."

My heart dropped into my stomach. My puppy-dog eyes were my superpower. But they never worked on Mrs. E.

Miss's face turned blotchy. "I—I should've asked. But I can't take it back. It's engraved."

A pink bubble of hope grew in my chest.

Mrs. E. folded her arms. The word for her look is *resigned*. "We'll let it go. This time. Keep it to yourself, Jacinta. No bragging."

But we *both* knew better. Bragging is what girls *do*.

I threw my arms around Miss. "Thank you!"

She staggered, then patted me on the back with the hand that wasn't pinned to her side.

"Are you rich?" I studied her face, but I could only see myself—as twins—reflected in her sunglasses.

Her smile crept up her cheek. As if I'd said something funny. Later she'd explain that people don't ask each other how much money they have. It's too *personal*. But I'd never heard of *personal*.

Mrs. Espinosa squeezed my shoulder. So I let go of Miss.

Then Mrs. E. said to her, "Thanks for your report on Teen Promise. We're already getting calls and donations."

Miss made what's called a *rueful* smile. "Then it wasn't a complete disaster. Most of the time it's just work, but this story really got to me. These girls are too young. We need to be there for them."

"We're glad you—oh! Wait!" Mrs. Espinosa dug into her purse and pulled out an envelope. "I knew there was reason for seeing you. I heard you love gymnastics. Didn't you compete when you were younger?"

"Until I got too tall."

"Here. Two passes for the exhibition tonight at Michener. A thank-you from the youth center."

For a moment, Miss's eyes brightened. "Eva Chávez is going to be there!" Then she frowned. "But the station has a strict policy about gratuities, and—the past few weeks haven't gone so well."

Miss sighed, and I knew. She had pain in her life. I knew because—since Mamá left—I'd had pain in mine. Maybe it's weird for a kid to feel sorry for a rich lady.

But I did.

Mrs. E. grinned. Pushing the envelope into Miss's hands, her voice dripped with syrupy sweetness. "Please take one of our girls. As a volunteer."

"Take me!" I didn't know I was going to say it. The words just popped out.

Mrs. E.'s eyes twinkled. "It's *community service.*"

Miss bit her lip. She looked at the envelope, then at me. Like I was a book she was trying to read. I showed her my puppy-dog eyes.

"I can't be your mentor," Miss warned.

Mrs. Espinosa's smile was warm, persuasive.

"You said that it's important to be there for these girls."

Miss made her sideways smile. A whiff of air blew out of her nose. Like a snort, only quiet.

Mrs. E. pressed. "Jacinta's family lives a few blocks away. I'll meet you there tonight to introduce you to her father."

Miss shrugged. "A one-time thing. Why not?"

Right now, I can think of a hundred reasons *why not.*

But that's how it started. By forgetting Mamá's sweater, I stepped onto a roller coaster—an *emotional* roller coaster.

I did it to myself.

And that just shows that the big wounds are *self-inflicted.*

3
CAPÍTULO TRES

I DIDN'T SPEND the afternoon being *apprehensive.* I didn't know that word.

Instead, Suelita and I bounced on the sofa. With every jump, white stuffing spilled out of the rips. We couldn't have done it if Mamá had been home.

Papi didn't notice.

He paced over the spot in the carpet where you could see the concrete underneath. Then he'd glance out the living-room window, into the dark stairwell.

Papi hadn't left for his night job. He wanted to meet the rich lady who was taking me somewhere. Rosa pretended to read one of my movie magazines.

When I stopped jumping to breathe, Papi asked me again, in Spanish. "What have you told this woman?"

"*Nada, Papi*"—nothing.

If it'd been up to him, I wouldn't be going with Miss at all. Papi liked everything to stay the same. That was the way to be safe. But Mamá had called that afternoon, so I'd been able to ask her if I could go with Miss. She was almost as excited as me. "Maybe this lady will be your Amiga, *mija!*"

When she said it, I'd crossed my fingers. For good luck.

Two pairs of legs came down the steps. I leaped off the sofa and threw open the door. Miss walked in first. She didn't need to duck, but she did. She looked bright and shiny in our dark apartment. If it'd been December, we could've put her in the window for a Christmas tree.

Suelita ran behind Papi and hung on to his pant leg. She scowled at Miss, practically growling. At age two, she already knew to be afraid of white people.

But Mrs. Espinosa was glowing. She was always trying to get new volunteers for the youth center.

Getting someone famous to volunteer was like having the prize show dog at the Durango Fair. "Miguel Juárez, this is Kath—"

Miss interrupted. "Call me Kate."

Papi took the pale hand she offered in his grease-stained one. He had to look up to nod to her. His face turned red under his dark skin. "Hello, Miss."

"How do you do, Miguel?" Her smile was so wide, I could've counted every one of her perfect teeth.

The ladies sat on our lumpy sofa. Papi's skin went darker. I don't know if it was because he hadn't asked them to sit, as Mamá would have, or because the cushions were covered in bits of fluff that stuck to their clothes.

You could've guessed Miss was a TV reporter, the way she started asking questions. "So, Jacinta, do you like school?"

"'S okay," I said, twisting my hair around a finger. *A lie.*

I hated school. Mamá would remind me that she'd left her own mother so that I could go to school. "You could be smart, *mija*! You could work in an office!" But office work was still work. I didn't see the point.

"What do you do for fun?" Miss asked.

"Watch movies. It's only three dollars on Tuesdays at the Costello."

"What kind of food do you like?"

"Tamales are my favorite. I don't like *gringo* food." Miss's lips twitched. Then I thought about cotton candy. "Maybe *some gringo* food."

Mrs. E.'s eyebrows traveled way up her forehead. "Jacinta, we don't say *gringo*. It's not a nice word."

My face got hot. I didn't know *gringos* don't like to be called *gringos*. I just thought it meant somebody who's not Mexican. Kids at school call us Mexicans sometimes. It's not a bad word either, but they use it like an insult — something meant to hurt.

Miss didn't look upset. Her smile hitched itself on the side of her face again. "I like Mexican food. But I'm not much of a cook. Maybe you'll teach me."

Happy butterflies in my stomach. She was talking *future tense.*

Rosa butted in. "I know how to cook, Miss! I can teach you!"

My Miss turned her sparkly eyes on Rosa, so my sister began to tell about the food she makes.

Both of them showed their big white teeth.

And the green monster grew in me.

The night started pretty bad. First I couldn't find Mamá's sweater. Miss kept looking at her watch while I dug through the front closet. She was tapping her foot by the time I remembered I'd shoved the sweater in my backpack on my way home. But I needed Mamá's sweater. For protection.

And I expected Miss to be driving something *cool*. Something I could brag to Angélica about at school the next day. I stood in the parking lot, looking around for a red sports car — maybe even a convertible. But when Miss pushed the button on her keychain, the lights flashed on an ugly brown minivan. What boys in our neighborhood would call a *beater*.

She wouldn't even let me sit in the front seat next to her. "The air bag could break your neck."

"I'll be twelve in two months!"

"My van, my rules."

Miss was being *annoying*—like Rosa—but annoying was familiar. I relaxed.

A little.

It'd started to rain, and it was already dark. And because we'd left late, Miss drove fast. Faster than Papi ever did. He needed to be careful. If *la policía* stopped him, he'd get a long bus ride and have to swim back.

The shiny black streets reflected the red glare of stoplights and taillights. Car dealerships and fast-food places flew by. My skin prickled at so much dangerous color.

Like having Christmas and a sick stomach at the same time.

I thought of Suelita and Rosa safe at home, snuggled together on the sofa, the soft light of the television bouncing off their faces in the dark.

But with Mamá gone, there's no one at home to cuddle me.

Everything in the van squeaked and rattled. The bare metal of the windshield wipers scraped half circles into the glass.

"You should have a red sports car."

"I need something to haul my kids around."

"How many kids do you have, Miss?"

"Two. Boys. A little older than you."

"If you were my Amiga, it'd be like having a daughter," I hinted.

The light ahead flicked from green to yellow to red. Miss's brakes squealed like an animal being stepped on. The sound made my teeth hurt. Even wearing my seat belt—which Miss had insisted on—I pitched forward.

While waiting for the light, she picked a piece of sofa stuffing from her skirt and flicked it away. Air from the heating vent caught it. The fluff floated up and attached itself to her shoulder. "Jacinta, why do you call me 'Miss'?"

"What else would I call you?"

"How about 'Kate'?"

"No, Miss. That wouldn't be polite."

She looked at me in the rearview mirror. "Then 'Miss' it is."

"How come you didn't work today?" I asked.

"I did."

"I watched 5News at Five. I didn't see you."

"They've got me doing features for the early-afternoon show."

"But you were at the youth center after school today."

"I finished early. I don't always have a live shot."

"Why not?"

She sighed. "Because some days they have real news."

That made me angry. Like maybe the stuff in my neighborhood wasn't important enough for TV.

Rosa always said I could talk the hind leg off a donkey, although talking its ears off would make more sense. But I couldn't think of anything else to say to Miss. I wasn't even sure I liked her that much. I was almost glad when she started asking questions again. Until I heard the question.

"Do you know what you want to be when you grow up?"

I knew what I *wanted* to be. I wanted to be a movie star. But kids in our neighborhood didn't get to be movie stars. So I just said, "No, Miss."

She nodded. "As long as it's not TV news."

"You don't like your job?"

"Let's just say I don't like the *environment*."

Back then I didn't understand what the *environment* had to do with Miss not liking her job. But now I know she just didn't like her boss.

We drove, not talking. I looked at the gum wrappers on the floor. "If *I* were rich, I'd buy a red convertible."

She made the small noise that was almost a snort. "So would I."

From behind came a siren. Red and blue lights bounced across the roof of the van. Panic.

"Oh, hell. I'm not speeding, am I?"

I couldn't speak. I wiped my damp hands on the seat.

The police car flew by and screamed away into the night. Relief flooded through me.

Miss said, "Thank goodness. We're late enough as it is."

4

CAPÍTULO
CUATRO

SHE DROVE into a *parking garage.*

I'd never been in one before. "Isn't that a lot of money to pay to park?"

"It's ridiculous, but all of the on-street parking is gone. *Somebody* wasn't ready when it was time to leave."

We climbed wide concrete steps to a big building. It *loomed.* Like a jail.

"Miss, what kind of meeting is this?" My voice sounded weird and high. I'd been so excited about going with Miss that I hadn't stopped to wonder where she was taking me.

"It's a *meet.* A gymnastics meet."

I stopped. "A *what?*"

Feeling me tug on her hand, Miss turned. Lights from the building outlined her *silhouette*. Her face was a shadow. "Gymnastics. It's a sport. Like — basketball. You know what basketball is?"

"Yesss." *Does she think I'm stupid?*

She started to move again. I yanked my hand away. "I don't know how to play."

Her teeth appeared in the dark. She was smiling. "We're not going to play. We're going to watch. It'll be fun."

I wasn't having fun. Miss smiled because I didn't know things. But I needed her to like me. When I'd talked to Mamá that afternoon, she'd reminded me that Angélica's Amiga bought her shoes. "You need new shoes, *mija*."

Heart pounding, I followed Miss inside.

Bright lights and the smell of nachos and pop-corn pushed away the gloom and damp. People glanced at us.

Then they looked again, gaping at Miss.

She didn't notice. She was used to being famous.

The lady taking tickets at the door of the large gymnasium spotted us. "Kathryn Dawson Dahl!"

She dragged Miss to the head of the line.

Heads turned. Instead of complaining about us taking cuts, people grinned. Some took pictures. Miss gave them her toothpaste smile. "Hello, everyone!"

"Is this your daughter?" asked the ticket lady.

"She's a friend," said Miss, still smiling for the cameras. So I did it, too. Like *I* was famous. I *had* been on television with her.

One of the men lowered his camera. "I'm glad you hired an attorney. That little blonde who replaced you is an airhead."

I looked at Miss. Her eyebrows strained to touch in the middle. It hurt my own face to watch her clinging to her smile. "We'd better get our seats."

"Goodness, yes! It's about to start." The ticket lady let us through, not bothering to take our passes.

Miss picked a row. As we squeezed past them, people pointed and whispered.

They think I'm the daughter of someone famous?

We plopped into seats as the lights went out.

"Ladies and gentlemen!" A game-show kind of voice echoed from the space above the crowd.

"Michener University presents the postseason Women's Gymnastics Exhibition!"

Sparklers exploded around the gym.

I jumped.

Girls wearing big smiles and tight, glittery black-and-yellow costumes bounced out of the dark. The girls flipped and flitted across the arena like bright little birds. *Gymnastics is nothing like basketball!*

The voice boomed again. "Featuring all-around winner of this year's N-C-double-A Gymnastic Championships! EVA CHÁVEZ!"

People leaped to their feet, yelling. We hopped up, too, but I couldn't see over the lady in front.

"Stand on the bench!" Miss shouted.

So I did.

A brown girl stood in a light of her own. She was smaller than me, and almost as dark. The crowd cheered. Eva Chávez smiled and waved. Everyone sat down, but the noise continued. I slipped onto the seat and pulled on Miss's sleeve.

"Is she famous?" I yelled.

Miss shouted back, "She's going to the Olympics."

I felt dizzy and happy. Like the cheering was for me.

Imagine girls flying without wings. That's gymnastics. Like dancing in the air.

Like *magic*.

Driving through the dark on the way home, Miss yawned, but I couldn't have slept if you'd paid me a million dollars. The entire night had been a happy dream.

Even without a sports car, Miss would make the best Amiga ever.

Better than Angélica's Amiga, who wore glasses on a chain and smelled like baby powder.

I clutched my new Michener Mountaineers T-shirt. The gymnasts had thrown them into the crowd. Miss jumped on the bench to catch one. Then she gave it to *me*.

As we drove past a streetlamp, I held up the shirt, trying to catch some light in the darkness. I wanted to read again the words written on it.

Miss had interviewed Eva Chávez on TV once,

so I got to meet her after the gymnastics. She kissed me. On both cheeks. Then across my new T-shirt, she wrote:

Para mi amiga Jacinta
♡ Eva Chávez

Somebody famous wrote that *I* was her *friend*.
She even had a Spanish name. Like me.
"Miss, how did Eva learn to do that stuff?"
"She's been training since she was little. Younger than you."
Younger than me? Could I flip around on skinny bars and walk across a narrow board? Would everyone cheer and call my name?
"I'd like to be a gymnast." Two hours before, I hadn't known the word *gymnast*. There I was telling Miss I wanted to be one.
But when Miss dropped me off, all she said was, "It was nice meeting you."
Past tense.
Nothing about being my Amiga, or seeing me again. The movie in my head ended *without* the princess getting the glass slipper.

When I walked inside, Rosa was slouched in front of the television. She looked up *expectantly*.

I didn't shove my T-shirt in her face. I didn't say anything about Eva Chávez, or sparklers, or even cotton candy. I went into our room and slammed the door.

SUELITA wasn't in the stroller—she was inside our apartment, having her diaper changed—so I didn't care if the stupid thing broke. The night before had been so big, so wonderful, but it hadn't changed anything. I let the stroller bang on every step as I dragged it up the stairwell.

At the top, grimy boots waited for me. Inside the grimy boots were the grimy feet of our apartment manager, Mr. Spitz. I *assumed* his feet were grimy. I lowered my eyes, glad not to look at his dirty T-shirt and fat belly.

"Hey, Rosa, where's your folks?"

"I'm Jacinta."

"Whatever."

"Mamá and Papi are working." This wasn't a lie. Mamá just wasn't getting paid.

He leaned toward me, and I smelled his chewing-tobacco breath. "Tell them to get the rent to my office, pronto."

He didn't scare me. We could never be evicted again. Papi had *two* jobs now. "Yes, Mr. Spit."

"*Spitz!*" He waddled away.

"What did he want?" Rosa carried Suelita, who wiggled to get down.

"Money."

Since Mamá wasn't around to clean houses, Papi sometimes had to avoid Mr. Spitz. But Papi worked a lot, and Mr. Spitz worked only when he felt like it, so avoiding him was easy.

Rosa inspected the stroller. "If you break it, you will carry Suelita to the food bank."

"Why do I even have to come?"

"Why are you so lazy?"

"Maybe the food bank isn't open."

"Tía said it is open." Rosa wheeled our sister down the driveway. I sighed and followed.

Tía Carmen always knew what days the food

bank was open. Our aunt had two little kids and another baby on the way. She watched Suelita while Rosa and I went to school.

When Mamá was home, she and Carmen traded caring for Suelita and my cousins so they could both work cleaning houses. Having Mamá gone was hard on our aunt, too, since she had to stay home with the babies and couldn't make money. Tía's boyfriend, Victor, was sometimes too "sick" to work.

It was a long walk to the food bank. Summer hadn't started, but somebody forgot to tell the weatherman. Sunshine bounced off the windshields of the cars speeding by, right into my eyes. I dragged a hand across my wet forehead.

The food bank stood behind a church with colored windows. To get there we had to cross *la línea* — the line. Americans lived on the other side. I didn't like crossing *la línea,* but white people didn't care if we went to the food bank. As long as we kept moving.

But once, Angélica's cousin and some of his friends were just hanging around in the *barrio blanco* — the white neighborhood — and somebody called *la policía*.

When I told Papi about it, he said hanging out in the *barrio blanco* is just asking for trouble. I couldn't understand why anyone would want to hang around the white neighborhood, anyway.

In our barrio you'd find your neighbors in the parking lot or on their porches, smoking or talking. Music poured from the open windows of pickup trucks. Kids laughed and shouted, chasing each other up and down the apartment staircases.

You never saw people in the white neighborhood. Sometimes a dog barked, but mostly it was quiet. Like a neighborhood full of dead people.

When we got close to the food bank, though, we heard music. Rosa and I looked at each other. We walked faster. The music got louder. We were almost running. Suelita leaned forward, her feet kicking the footrest as the stroller bumped over the cracks in the sidewalk.

The church parking lot was usually empty, but a million kids were crowded around the 5News truck as it pumped out music. The same camera guy took video while a mob swarmed around Miss as she signed autographs.

I pushed into the horde, trying to reach her. "Miss!"

She didn't look up from the picture she was signing.

"MISS KATE!"

Her head came up. Her real smile inched up the side of her face. She nodded at me. Then she went back to signing her name.

It was enough. I wasn't like every other kid, begging for her autograph. I was her *friend*. And I didn't need her name on a photo to prove it.

But I got one anyway.

To show Angélica.

Rosa took Suelita inside to get our food, but I stayed in the scorching parking lot while Miss did her *live shot*. A bunch of us kids stood behind her and waved at the camera while Miss interviewed Miss Ordaz, the food-bank lady.

When the guy put his camera away, the crowd disappeared, but I stayed to watch Miss help him pack up. She struggled with a supersize suitcase that must've weighed a bazillion tons. "I'm too old for this."

He said, "So quit. You have enough years to retire."

"Two kids to put through college, and my ex's alimony? The only one who gets to retire is my lawyer."

Miss turned and gave me that sideways smile. Then her eyes moved to Rosa, who'd walked up next to me. Suelita hung on to her arm. Our food was piled in the stroller. Miss's smile flickered. "You girls want a ride?"

Cool! "In the TV truck?"

"No, in my van. I'm on my way home."

Oh. Not so cool. "Sure, Miss."

"Excuse me?"

"Sure," I repeated.

Rosa elbowed me. So I said, "Thank you, Miss."

Instead of saying, "You're welcome," Miss just said, "Better."

She opened the back of her ugly brown van so I could shove our food inside.

Suelita fought and cried while Rosa strapped her

into a fold-down toddler seat. My baby sister didn't want to go with Miss, and she didn't like seat belts.

"Didn't you say your boys are *older* than me?" I asked.

"That shows you how long I've had this van," said Miss.

Rosa got to sit in front because she was fourteen. I got stuck in back with Suelita, who continued to scream, right in my ear. So when Miss pulled out of the parking lot, I didn't hear what she'd said. But Rosa laughed.

The green beast clawed at my insides. I pushed the button to let Suelita out of the car seat so she'd stop crying. She scrambled onto the floor of the van.

Just as fast, Miss pulled to the side of the road. "Not okay."

She got out, threw open the side door, and caught Suelita, who howled and screamed. Miss wrestled her back into the booster seat. My eyes popped. Suelita was *the baby*. We always let her have her way.

Rosa said, "Miss! I can hold her in my lap."

Struggling with Suelita, who continued shrieking, Miss panted. "Not good enough. Have you seen what happens in an accident to a kid not wearing a seat belt? I have. It goes with the job."

Just as the buckle clicked, Suelita's hard little shoe caught Miss right in the nose. Miss's hand came up to her face. She staggered backward. Suelita cheered. Miss slammed the door, then pulled herself into her own seat. She inspected her face in the rearview mirror.

Rosa swallowed. "Your nose, Miss. It is bleeding."

"Yeah, I noticed that." Her voice sounded stuffy. I unbuckled my belt and slid forward to see. Miss dug through her purse, coming up with some tissues, but blood dripped onto her shiny blouse.

"It's getting on your clothes," I said.

Miss grabbed at her blouse. The air in her lungs escaped in a groan.

When we got to our apartment, Rosa invited Miss to come in and wash off the blood. As Suelita was carried inside, I saw her exchange looks with

Miss over Rosa's shoulder. The word for those looks is *animosity*.

On both sides.

Rosa took Suelita into our parents' room to change her diaper again, while Miss stood at the kitchen sink, dousing her blouse with cold water.

"You're getting all wet," I told her.

"It feels good. It's nice and cool down here — the advantage of a garden-level apartment."

I'd never heard of a *garden-level apartment*. I couldn't wait to tell Angélica, who told everybody that I lived in a basement.

Then Miss handed me food to go in the cupboard. *A rich lady helping put groceries away?*

When I thanked her, she said, "My pleasure. I'm not looking forward to going back out in that heat. Good thing I'm taking the boys swimming."

Swimming? I stared at Miss with puppy-dog eyes.

Her face went tomato red. "I shouldn't have said that right in front of you. It was rude."

I didn't speak. Except with my eyes.

A fly buzzed around the room and landed on the screen door.

Miss cleared her throat. "Would—your dad let you go with us?"

I grinned. Taking me swimming wasn't something she wanted to do. Miss seemed tough. But I'd found her weakness.

6 CAPÍTULO SEIS

ROSA DUCKED to look in Abuelita's mirror so the crack in the glass wouldn't cut across her forehead. She pouted, reaching for her lip gloss.

I wanted to smack her.

At the gymnastics meet, Miss *reapplied* her lipstick after we ate cotton candy. But when I asked her to put some on me, she'd refused. I told Rosa. "Miss says makeup is *inappropriate* for little girls."

Rosa's eyes flicked over to me sprawled on my bed. "I am not a little girl."

Smiling into the mirror, she pulled at her T-shirt, admiring the way it hugged her shape.

If I'd been a cartoon, steam would've blasted out my ears.

Miss's sons—rich white boys—would go crazy for Rosa, with her lighter skin and movie-star eyes. I didn't care about *them,* but I didn't need Rosa butting in. "Maybe Miss won't want her sons hanging around a *Mexican.*"

"I am not the one who called her a *gringa,*" Rosa shot back.

I gasped like she'd thrown ice water in my face. I stomped out, slamming the door, and joined Tía Carmen, Suelita, and my cousins in the living room.

When Rosa called Papi at work, he worried about us going swimming with Miss's sons. He reminded us again what happened to Tía Carmen before she dropped out of school. All because *los muchachos sólo desean una cosa*—boys only want one thing.

Papi didn't say what it was boys wanted, but I already knew. Parents in the barrio worried about girls getting pregnant. But it wasn't something they'd talk about.

Especially fathers.

Especially Papi.

And there was another problem. Suelita wasn't invited. Miss said she wasn't comfortable trying to supervise four older kids *and* a toddler at the same time.

Rosa promised to watch Suelita, but Miss said no, there would be too many *distractions* at the pool. Miss said she had our little sister's *safety* to consider.

I think Miss was *considering* that Suelita had kicked her in nose.

With Mamá away, Papi wasn't sure what to do, so he called his sister, Carmen. Even more than having her watch Suelita, Papi wanted Tía Carmen to meet the dangerous boys who'd be with us in the water wearing nothing but their swimsuits — tall, handsome, rich boys that no girl could resist. Boys who could get Rosa and me "into trouble."

Maybe Papi thought our aunt's pregnant belly would be a warning to Miss's sons.

Tía was happy to come. Our apartment was cooler than hers. But she told me to be back by seven. Victor would get angry if she didn't have dinner waiting when he'd had to work late. I told her I'd remember.

I really thought I'd remember.

A stampede of legs came down the stairwell. I ran to open the door. When Tía Carmen stood, Suelita and my cousins ran to hide behind her.

"Hi, Jacinta." Miss gave me a quick one-armed hug. *A thrill all the way to my toes.* I hated that she had so much power over me.

Then Miss gave my aunt a little wave. "*Hola . . .* Carmen?"

Tía smoothed her dress over where her baby was starting to show. "*Hola,* Miss Kate."

"These are my sons, Ethan and Cody."

They shuffled in, watching their feet, their hands in their pockets. There's a word for how they looked. *Scruffy.*

Not scary. *Scared.* And skinny. And short.

I couldn't help it. Laughter bubbled out of me. The boys looked at each other. Tía Carmen laughed, too. She could tell Papi that our hearts wouldn't be stolen.

Rosa swept into the room, ready to meet her prince. Love at first sight. Like in the movies. When she saw Miss's sons, she stopped. Her eyebrows came together, and her mouth fell open.

I grinned. If I'd been a cartoon, devil horns would've been poking up through my hair.

Ethan, the older boy, called "Shotgun!" which meant he got to sit in front with Miss. So Rosa and I claimed the middle seat. The younger boy, Cody, sat behind us.

"Seat belts," said Miss. Then she steered her van in the *opposite* direction of the pool.

Rosa and I looked at each other. I said, "You're going the wrong way, Miss."

She snorted. Not a pig sound. Just that ladylike puff of air. "I'm pretty sure I can get there without help."

The van rumbled away from our barrio, burping up clouds of blue smoke. In minutes nothing looked familiar. There were stores I knew the names of, but I didn't recognize the buildings. *Where's she taking us?* My mouth went dry. I couldn't have spit if you'd paid me a million dollars.

"Is this okay?" Rosa whispered to me.

"Sure." But I crossed my fingers.

Long after we should've been at the pool, we took another turn. Then we were on a *freeway*.

I gripped Rosa's hand. Her *sweaty* hand.

We'd been places in Papi's truck, but never on the freeway. Driving on a freeway is like begging *la policía* to drag you back to Mexico. The only times we'd been on a freeway were to go to Abuelita's farm. For that we'd taken a big, slow bus.

But Miss had been driving for a long time. *Too long, too far, too fast.* My heart beat like bongos.

Eyes wide, Rosa pointed. A sign said PHOENIX SCHOOL OF TECHNOLOGY.

I tried to swallow but couldn't. One of Papi's brothers lived in Phoenix. In *Arizona.* We lived in Colorado. If we were in Phoenix, it could mean only one thing: Miss—who might have been watching us in the rearview mirror through her dark glasses— had taken us across state lines, like Mamá always warned about.

Miss would sell us into slavery.

Speaking in Spanish, I said to Rosa, "Is Miss kidnapping us?"

Rosa squeezed my hand, hard enough to hurt. "Would she do that in front of her sons?"

"Maybe the boys will force us into cages!"

Rosa frowned. "We're bigger than they are."

Miss said in a tired voice, "Ladies, it's impolite to speak Spanish if people with you can't understand it."

My blood turned icy.

Rosa whispered, still in Spanish, "Should we jump?"

I gulped. Miss's van whizzed by the other cars. On TV, when people jump from moving vehicles, they *roll*. So they don't get squished. But I wasn't sure if it would work in real life. "Wait until she slows down."

The van pulled away from the lanes of traffic. Quietly I unbuckled my seat belt and looked at Rosa, my hand on the door. Rosa unbuckled her belt, then grabbed the other handle. The van rolled into a parking lot. I nodded to Rosa.

Ready to run, we yanked on our door handles.

They didn't open.

Just two dull thunks.

My arm went limp. I looked at Rosa. Her face reminded me of the time Angélica fainted in health class when the teacher explained the reproductive system.

"Girls, wait until I stop." Miss sounded bored.

The van eased into a parking space, and Miss shut off the engine. Her younger son reached around to tug at the door on Rosa's side.

"Cody, let the girls out first," said Miss.

"Mom, you've got the locks on."

"Oh. Sorry." She punched a button, and the locks clicked.

Cody slid the door open. With a sweep of his hand, he motioned for Rosa to go first. Like a guy in a movie.

We staggered, like we were getting off a ride at the amusement park. Rosa's skin is usually light brown, but just then her face was yellow. "W-where are we?"

"At the rec center." Miss turned to look at her. "Honey, are you carsick?"

Rosa shook her head but said nothing.

The sign over the door of the building read SOUTH MAPLEWOOD RECREATION CENTER.

We drove all this way and we're still in Maplewood? "Miss, why'd it take so long to get here?"

She glanced at her watch. "It's rush hour."

My legs were still watery when we walked inside.

I stopped, gaping. This place looked nothing like the pool we normally went to. The recreation center was a ginormous, gleaming glass donut. The swimming pool was in the middle—right where the donut hole would be.

Every minute a big green tube—a waterslide— dumped a different kid into the pool with a splash. There were fountains and sprays and waterfalls.

"Miss, how rich do you have to be to come here?" My voice was *hushed*. Like at church.

Miss frowned. "I'm not rich. This is a public building."

"Can I help the next person?" called the girl behind the counter.

Miss handed her a credit card.

"Miss, don't you have to be *rich* to have a credit card?"

She made another wheezy snort, and I realized that's how she laughed. "No, but a credit card can make you poor."

"Miss, when you smile like that, your mouth goes over to the side of your face."

"They call that a smirk."

Smirk. I liked that word. It had the right sound for Miss's sideways smile.

Miss's boys wrestled with each other while the girl swiped Miss's credit card. Ethan's red hair hung into his eyes. His clothes were wrinkled, like he'd slept in them. He pretended to choke his little blond brother.

Cody faked like he was dying. The glasses he wore made him look smart instead of nerdy—or they would have if his tongue hadn't been sticking out and his eyes hadn't been crossed.

Rosa and I giggled.

Signing the credit card slip, Miss said in her tired voice, "Ethan, stop manhandling your brother."

Manhandling. That was a good word, too. I

liked that about Miss. Her words. The way she juggled them.

Sun streamed in the many windows. People exercised to bouncy music. Water from the fountains in the pool glittered like diamonds. It was all busy and happy, like nothing could ever be wrong again.

7

WE'D NEVER BEEN to an indoor pool. It's noisy. The sounds bounce all around and jump back at you. The air is wet, hard to breathe, and smells like the janitor's cleaning stuff. We stood at the water's edge, sweating. Not just from the heat.

Aside from Rosa and me, there wasn't one Mexican at the pool. And everyone else wore swimsuits. We usually just swam in shorts and a T-shirt.

We watched Miss's boys dunk each other, laughing. Ethan didn't look like he could be in high school. Cody—who was one grade ahead of me—was so tiny that even Ethan could throw him around.

Cody would land with a splash, come up grinning, and push back through the water to Ethan, who'd throw him again.

Maybe Ethan will throw me in the water! I hoped so. Rosa never played with me in the pool. She would flip and swirl — underwater — the whole time. She didn't even have to breathe. She looked like she was dancing, her eyes open and everything. Papi called her his Little Mermaid.

But we were shy. There were white boys at school, but they never talked to us. *What if Ethan and Cody don't like us?* I looked at Rosa.

She shrugged and stepped into the pool. I followed, enjoying the cool water moving past my legs.

A sharp trill broke the air. The lifeguard waved us over, taking the whistle out of her mouth. She wasn't much older than Rosa. "Girls, you can't swim without suits."

My heart belly-flopped into my stomach.

Rosa cringed. Like she'd been slapped. "We grew out of them."

"I'm sorry. Those are the rules." The lifeguard didn't seem sorry. She chewed her gum and swung her whistle back and forth. I hoped she knew CPR, because I was having a heart attack.

"Is there a problem?" Miss's voice. My heart jumped back to life.

The lifeguard's eyes widened. "Aren't you—?"

Miss gave a nod and something like a smile. Her mouth turned up at the corners, but her lips were thin, and her eyes didn't sparkle. "Kathryn Dawson Dahl."

I'd only heard Miss tell people to call her Kate. Why would she tell someone all three of her names? The lifeguard flapped her hands like she was doing the chicken dance. "My mom watches you all the time!"

I told Miss, "She says we can't go swimming!"

"We do not have swimsuits," Rosa added. For once it was her, and not me, whose eyes were leaking.

The lifeguard blurted, "It's okay. Just for today."

Rosa and I grinned at each other. I felt light. Pink soap bubbles floating over blue water.

Miss gave another smile-that-wasn't-a-smile to the lifeguard. "I appreciate it."

She'd used her name in a way I'd never seen before. A name is something to be called, but sometimes a teacher would use a name as a threat. *Do you want to visit Principal Stroud?*

Or a name can be a warning. *¡Ven aquí, Jacinta Juárez Castro!* When Mamá said *come here* and used all of my names, I was in trouble.

But this was the first time I'd heard a name used as a *tool*. In my mind I saw Papi using a crowbar on a smashed car at the auto-body shop. Miss used her name to pry open a door.

There's a word for that. It's called *leverage*.

Without knowing the word, I knew that's what I needed. Something I could use to make Miss my Amiga.

Leverage.

YOU'D THINK that hungry girls who'd been swim-ming all afternoon would find *something* in a menu as big as a book.

But that was just it. The menu was *too* big. I was used to menus hanging on a wall.

The cover of this menu read:

Mom's Diner
"Shut up and eat!"

For someone so worried about politeness, I was surprised Miss would take us to a place where the menu was rude. But the girl who served us was nice. She wanted to take our order, but Rosa and I couldn't decide. She said she'd give us "a few minutes."

But it'd been more than a few minutes.

Miss sighed. "Ladies, it's dinner, not brain surgery."

My face burned. *We should've gone someplace normal. Where food comes in paper bags, handed through a window to your car.*

The boys were sword fighting with their straws.

"Guys," said Miss in her tired voice. The one Ethan called the *Nag-O-Matic.*

He made a huffing sound, but they stopped. Ethan and Cody weren't snobby, even though they were rich. They were the *opposite* of snobby, but I didn't know the word for that.

The word is *inclusive.*

And even that sounds too snobby for the Dahl boys.

At the pool they showed us how to play Marco Polo. And we had a water fight. I could dunk Cody, but not Ethan. Not by myself, anyway.

The server girl came back to our table with coloring papers and crayons.

"How about some kids' menus?"

Miss looked relieved.

When the girl walked away, I asked Miss again, "Will the recreation center really let me take gymnastics for free?"

After we'd finished swimming, Miss had led Rosa and me down the hall to the gymnastics room while Ethan and Cody played in the recreation center's arcade.

The gymnastics room was big enough to be its own building. Girls flew through the air in every direction. I had to be one of them.

With puppy-dog eyes on maximum power, I focused on Miss. She got me a *scholarship application* at the center's front desk.

A free class? For real? I couldn't stop talking about it during the drive to the restaurant, so Miss got annoyed when I brought it up again. "We'll *see.* Have your dad fill out the form."

But Papi would want me to wait until Mamá got home. Who knew when that would be?

And there was something else.

"How would I get to gymnastics, Miss? Papi has to work nights." *Days, too.*

Miss hesitated.

Puppy-dog eyes.

She said, "Maybe I could drive you when we go swimming. Just until you make some car-pool friends."

My heart did a triple flip.

My sister tied the paper wrapper from her straw into knots. Miss noticed. "Rosa, do you want to take gymnastics, too?"

"No, Miss. No, thank you."

We couldn't both take gymnastics. One of us would have to watch Suelita.

It's only fair. I found Miss first.

The girl came back for our food order. She wrote everything down, then thanked us and walked away.

"She's nice."

"Who?" Miss asked me.

"That girl."

"What girl?"

"The server girl. The one who brought the crayons."

"You mean the *waitress*?" Ethan's laugh broke over me, loud and sharp. I scowled. How was I supposed to know the English word for *mesera* if I'd never been in a restaurant?

A smile tickled Miss's cheek, but she told Ethan, "That's enough."

He laughed until tears leaked out his eyelids. The water in my eyes wasn't from laughing. *How can someone so nice be so mean? And Miss is smiling, too. Smiling because I don't know stuff.*

Blood rushed to my face. Under the table Rosa took my hand and squeezed. I decided—right then—Miss would be my Amiga, no matter what I had to do. Not because I liked her.

Just then I hated her.

But I would follow her, like a greedy goose at the park. I would gobble her words like bits of tortilla. My brain would grow so fat that no one would ever laugh at me again.

Miss dropped us off in front of our apartment. She couldn't see down the stairwell, so she never knew about the broken glass outside our front door. Rosa and I picked our way through the shards.

Our front window was shattered.

Papi emerged with a broom and a trash can. His face was hard. I was afraid and relieved to see him.

"You are late," he said in Spanish.

"*¿Qué pasó?*" asked Rosa.

"Carmen told you to be back by seven." His voice was a knife.

Rosa swallowed. "No, Papi. Tía did not say that."

I dropped my eyes. "*Sí.* She told me."

Then I glanced up. Papi's look was sharp. I stepped back, feeling the glass crunch under my flip-flops.

Papi said, "When Carmen wasn't home to make Victor's dinner, he came looking for her. He was drunk. He broke our window when she wouldn't open the door."

I imagined Victor's angry face, the crooked scar on his eyelid. Most of the people in our neighborhood never caused trouble. No one wanted *la policía* to come. But Victor was what Papi called *una oveja negra* — a black sheep. I swallowed. "Is Tía okay?"

"She took him to the hospital. He cut his hand on the glass."

"Suelita?" Rosa's voice sounded small.

"She's in your bed, along with your cousins. I had to leave work."

"Sorry, Papi," I whispered.

He pointed at me. "Tomorrow I have to fix the window before Mr. Spitz sees. Do you know how much that will cost?"

Tears rolled down. "No, Papi."

"I don't get paid when I don't work. Mr. Spitz needs his money. He has a family, too."

I didn't think of that. That someone like Mr. Spitz could have a family. I wiped my face with my hands. "Sorry, Papi."

"Sorry isn't enough. We need money to pay for Abuelita's medicine. We need money for your *mamá* to come home. Don't you want to see her? Don't you want your *abuelita* to get well?"

"Yes, Papi," I sobbed.

"You girls shouldn't be out with strangers when your family needs you. No more going out with Miss."

"No, Papi! Please!"

"No more going to the youth center. For either of you." He started sweeping the broken glass.

Rosa turned on me. There's a word for her look. *Malice.*

I'd forgotten the first rule of being Mexican. *Family comes first.*

CAPÍTULO NUEVE

AFTER SCHOOL the next day, us girls crowded around Angélica. My heart thrummed in my ears—a drumroll. Like a magic trick, Angélica whipped out the phone her Amiga had bought for her. Pink jewels covered the case.

Angélica pretended to be bored, which was totally fake. "Miss Linda knows she's not supposed to buy me stuff, but she *has* to be able to get ahold of me."

What would it be like to have an Amiga who cared so much whether she could reach me? The green beast in my belly kicked. I swallowed a moan.

Walking home from school, Miss's supersize smile on the billboard *taunted* me. Angélica's eyes followed mine to the sign. "Has she called you?"

I hadn't said anything to Angélica about the night before. I hadn't wanted her to know that Papi said we couldn't go to the youth center anymore. I was still trying to find a way out of it. So I shrugged, examining my flip-flops as I dragged my feet across the pavement.

Angélica grinned. But I heard the smirk in her voice. *"¡Qué pena!"*—what a shame!

My head shot up. "I went swimming with her last night. She brought her two sons. Then we had dinner. In a *restaurant*."

She studied me, trying to decide if I was lying. I didn't blink. She yanked out her glittery phone. "Call her."

"She's at work."

"I call my Amiga at work."

"I don't have the number."

Rolling her eyes, she pressed a few numbers into the phone, then spoke into it. "Denver, Colorado. 5News." *Pause.* "The newsroom."

Then she shoved the phone at me.

My heart fluttered like bird wings while I listened to the phone ringing.

A man's voice. "5News. Maury Carlson."

"Can I — is Miss Kate there?" I croaked.

"Who?"

"Kathryn Dawson Dahl."

"She's about to do a live shot. Can you call back?"

Disappointment and relief crashed in on me. "Okay, bye."

I handed the phone to Angélica. I kept my voice *casual*. "She's about to do a *live shot*. On *television*."

Enjoying the look on her face, I added, "I'm gonna watch. See you later."

I hopped down our stairwell.

Papi had been replacing the broken window when I'd left for school. But he was gone, and the new glass looked clean and shiny. It was Rosa's day to pick up Suelita from Tía Carmen's. I was alone. Grabbing the remote, I clicked to channel five.

A man with a tie and a blond lady took turns telling the news. A building burned down. A *suspect* got shot in a robbery. But nothing about Miss. I worried I'd missed her or that Rosa would come home before I got a chance to see her.

Papi didn't say we couldn't watch Miss on TV.

But I looked over my shoulder, out the window at the stairwell, feeling guilty.

"5*News First Look* continues its series on immigration." My head swung back to the television to watch the man with the tie. "The Maplewood city council plays host this afternoon to a naturalization ceremony. Here with the story is 5News's Kathryn Dawson Dahl."

Her face took up the whole screen. "Steve, today marks the end of a long road for these immigrants. Naturalization is costly, tedious, and often risky. The process is shrouded in mystery, especially for those whose first language is *not* English."

Her concerned look froze. In my mind I heard a man say, *"Take video."* Then Miss told about a Costa Rican woman who was becoming a citizen after living in the U.S. for twelve years with her American husband.

Twelve years? As long as I've been alive.

The Costa Rican lady cried, talking about how much she loved America. A lump grew in my throat.

Then Miss was back, clutching her microphone. "We'll wrap up this series at North Middle School, where test scores remain high in the face of a large immigrant enrollment. That's tomorrow, on 5*News First Look.*"

The man with the tie came back on, but I couldn't hear what he said. *My school! Miss is coming to my school!* Deep inside me, a tiny voice starting singing.

"I know what you're thinking."

I jumped. Rosa stood in the open doorway. She dropped Suelita's hand, crossed the room to take the remote from me, and snapped off the television. "It will not work. I'll tell Papi."

I twisted my hair around my finger. "I don't know what you're talking about."

But I worried all night that Rosa would ruin my new secret plan.

The next morning I was lucky. Rosa and Suelita were both sick and throwing up.

Rosa's scratchy voice *penetrated* the new windowpane as I climbed the stairs. "You better be walking home!"

I raced to school, not waiting for Angélica. I

scanned the parking lot for the 5News truck. *Where is she?* I sat on the curb.

The first bell rang. I wiped my soggy hands on my shorts. Angélica ran by with her nose in the air, pretending she didn't see me.

I decided to give up just before the second bell rang. I was late. When I got to homeroom, our teacher wrote my name on the board for detention.

I spent the rest of that morning darting down hallways between classes, craning my neck, searching for Miss. *Her series ends today! If I don't find her, how will I ever get another chance?*

At lunch I checked the parking lot, praying for the news truck to be there. *Yes!* I charged back inside. Hesitating in the main entry, I scanned the corridors, wondering which way to go, straining to hear her TV voice.

Mr. Stroud came out of his office.

My cheeks got hot, like all my blood cells got called to an emergency meeting in my head. For once I was glad my skin was dark. Maybe the principal wouldn't notice my guilty face.

He stopped. "Jacinta, isn't it?"

I nodded, staring at the floor.

"You've got detention this afternoon?"

I nodded again.

"Where are you supposed to be now?"

Water sprang to my eyes. *My secret plan. Ruined.* "Lunch."

"Then I suggest you head to the cafeteria."

I hurried, my head down. So people wouldn't see my tears.

Which is why I ran into Miss. Again.

"Jacinta?" Her voice was the sound of water trickling over rocks in a desert.

"Miss!" I forgot everything. My whole secret plan. I threw my arms around her and sobbed into her blouse.

Later that afternoon I scooted around our apartment like a jumping bean in the sun. If Rosa hadn't been sick, she would've known I was up to something.

But she kept dashing to the bathroom.

Papi was in his bedroom, getting ready for his

night job, and Rosa was throwing up, when Miss came down the stairwell. I waited for her knock.

Papi called out for me to get the door.

Pulling it open, I said in a loud voice, "Miss! What are you doing here?"

Papi emerged from the bedroom.

Miss said, "I'm sorry, Jacinta. I know you said not to come. But I felt *obligated*."

That word again. I worked to keep from grinning.

She looked at Papi. "May I sit down?"

"Please." He waved to the sofa. I sat between them.

Rosa staggered from the bathroom and collapsed into the chair, shooting me angry looks through bleary red eyes.

"Miguel, it's my fault your girls were late after swimming. Please don't blame them. Or the youth center. Your girls need structure. Jacinta needs the social support."

Structure? Social support? I just wanted an Amiga. I hoped Papi understood. Miss sounded like she'd eaten a dictionary for lunch.

Papi stiffened. "Thank you, Miss, but they have many things, here, to do."

I said. "It's okay, Miss. There are girls in our building. I can be friends with Isabel."

"No, you can't," Rosa croaked—as though I were stupid. "She got pregnant and went back to Mexico, remember?"

She couldn't have done it better if I'd paid her a million dollars. I looked from Papi to Miss, enjoying their faces when Rosa said "pregnant."

Controlling my own face, I said, "Maybe Lupe?"

Papi frowned. "I do not want you with Lupe. She goes with boys in fast cars."

I pulled my eyebrows together. "There are lots of *boys* in the building. They pay attention to me now that I'm older. Especially the high-school boys."

Miss went even more white. *Albino.*

I added, "But I'm becoming a *woman.* Without Mamá here, I need a *woman* to talk to."

Papi's brown skin looked green. "You have Rosa and Carmen."

My eyes started stinging for real. I blinked

and water spilled down my face. "Rosa will be in high school next year, and you and Tía are always working."

I had wanted Papi and Miss to *think* I was crying, but because the tears were real, I was embarrassed. I stared at the carpet, hiding my face with my hair. I felt Miss and Papi looking at each other over my head. I held my breath and crossed my fingers.

Papi coughed.

Miss cleared her throat. "Uh, Miguel, have you thought of enrolling Jacinta in the Amiga program?"

Behind my curtain of hair, a smirk crawled up the side of my face.

PAPI STARED at the paper, clicking the button on the end of the pen. The little point poked in and out.

Click.

Click.

The writing was English, so Papi wouldn't be hurried. There's a word for being slow like that. *Cautious.*

I picked at the peeling paint on the kitchen table, waiting in case he had questions. I'd just finished sixth grade and was the best reader in our family—in English—even though I didn't like reading.

Rosa would be going into high school, but she took ELA classes—English Language Acquisition. She was already nine when we moved back to

Colorado, so she spoke English with an accent. I spoke both English and Spanish with no accent.

But Rosa could read and write in Spanish, and I could not.

I chipped the polish off my fingernails and glanced at Papi. He reminded me of *mi abuelo*—my grandfather—after his accident.

Mi abuelo would stare at the fields, blowing smoke rings with his cigar. *Will there be enough rain? Will the crops survive?* Sometimes Abuelo would smile, and the corners of his eyes would crinkle like old paper. But mostly he was serious.

Even though my grandfather was my mother's father, Papi reminded me of him just then. He tapped the paper with his finger. *"¿Otra vez, qué es esto?"*—What is this again?

"It's for me to take *gymnastics*."

I tried to say the English word *lightly*. Like it was no big deal.

"Gymnastics?" Papi repeated in English.

I imagined myself doing things Eva Chávez did, people cheering and clapping. "Cartwheels . . . doing the splits."

Papi gave me the Spanish word. *"Gimnasia.* How much will it cost?"

"If you fill out the paper, it will be free."

Click went the pen. *Click.*

I wiped my wet hands on my shorts.

"Where did you get this paper?" he asked.

"Miss got it at the *recreation center.*" I said *recreation center* in English, because I didn't have the words to explain in Spanish. "Where the swimming pool is." Papi clicked the pen in and out. *I should've waited for Mamá to call. Mamá would've told Papi it's good to learn new things.*

But I realized my mistake too late.

Papi said, "This paper's from the city. They're asking how much money we have, where we live, how many people are in our family. It's not good to tell the government too much. That's the way to get a long bus ride. Then you have to swim back across the river."

I smiled. "You always say that."

"Because it's always true. Never forget that, *mija.*"

He rubbed my cheek with the back of his fingers as he said "my daughter." Then his eyes got big.

"What have you told *Miss* about our family?" He spoke Spanish except when he said *Miss*.

"Nothing, Papi."

He stared at me hard.

"I don't tell family things," I repeated.

The pen clicked again. And again.

"I need to think about this." He stood and picked up the paper.

I leaped from my chair. It fell backward. Papi had turned away, but when my chair slammed onto the floor, he spun around to face me.

"Mamá would let me take gymnastics!" I threw at him.

His eyes pierced me. I took a step back.

Then his face softened. "Jacinta, your *mamá* isn't here."

He left the gymnastics paper in the stack by the phone and walked out. The picture in my mind of doing gymnastics disappeared.

Like the smoke from *mi abuelo*'s last cigar.

She was smiling again because I didn't know things. I threw my words at her. "People will think I'm black!"

"First, there's nothing wrong with being black. People come in all colors. Second, your skin is perfect."

Miss was smart, but some things she couldn't understand. She didn't know that her creamy skin opened doors—doors that would slam in my face. I chose a two-piece suit that came with a swim shirt to go over it, so people wouldn't see my back.

We stood in line to buy it.

"Jacinta, keep this to yourself. About the swimsuit. Don't lie. Just—don't mention it. Promise?"

"I can't tell Mamá when she calls?"

Miss blushed. "I wouldn't ask you to keep a secret from your parents. I'd just rather this didn't get back to Liz Espinosa. But if you're coming to the rec center with us, you need a swimsuit. So please don't brag to your friends."

I coiled my hair around a finger. "Okay, Miss."

But it was too late.

Angélica had called that morning, inviting me to

11

IT WAS COLD in the fitting room. I felt like I was naked. I practically was.

"I don't like this one, Miss."

"You said you wanted a one-piece swimsuit?"

"Not this one. Look." I turned around and motioned with my hand.

"Your back?"

"Yesssss."

Miss sighed. "What don't you like?"

"I'm sunburned."

In the mirror her smirk crept across the opposite side of her face. "Dark skin doesn't mean you're burned."

join her and Miss Linda, going to the movies. I'd told Angélica I'd be shopping for a new swimsuit with my *own* Amiga. The famous one. Kathryn Dawson Dahl.

Sorry.

But I wasn't sorry. I'd used all three of Miss's names. As a weapon. I'd wanted to hurt Angélica, like she'd hurt me all those times, telling me about *her* wonderful Amiga. I didn't mention that Miss had agreed to be my Amiga only until her lawyer could force 5News to give her back her old job—reading the news on the anchor desk. Then Miss would be working nights, so she wouldn't be able to take me places after school.

I stood at her elbow while she paid for the suit. Then I remembered to be *gracious.* "Thank you, Miss. You're awesome."

She smirked. "The Grand Canyon is awesome, Jacinta. Save that word for when you need it."

Maybe *gracious* is something only kids have to be.

We were about to leave the store when Miss stopped. She stared at me. At my clothes. "Would you like a new sweater?"

I clutched Mamá's sweater. "No, Miss. No, thank you."

"Fine. But you'll need a new sweater for school this fall."

My stomach swooped. Like when you think an elevator is going up but it goes down instead. *Will Mamá be back before school starts?* Every week when she'd call, I'd ask her when she was coming home. She'd say, "I need to stay as long as Abuelita needs me."

I still wouldn't wash the sweater, even though it smelled like dirty socks instead of Mamá. I'd had to dig it out of the laundry hamper. Then I hid it under my mattress so Rosa wouldn't find it. It was wrinkled as well as grubby and smelly. But I needed to wear it until Mamá came home, no matter how long it took.

But it wasn't easy to say no to Miss. She didn't act like an *amiga*—a friend. She called herself my *mentor*. I wasn't even sure what it meant.

I wanted *reassurance*.

So as we walked through the mall, I took her hand and asked, "When can I go to your house?"

"*My* house?"

"I want to see it."

I listened to Miss's heels click across the tiles. "Jacinta, please don't take this the wrong way, but—I don't enjoy having guests. After working all week, I'm just not up to it."

I let go of her hand. But I don't think she noticed.

Her heels continued clicking on the hard tiles. "Will Rosa be back by the time we reach your place? I'd like to get her a swimsuit, too."

I'd said Rosa was with friends when Miss wanted to take us both shopping. Miss wasn't supposed to know we traded off babysitting Suelita while Papi worked.

Two years ago a white lady in our building called *la policía* because our neighbor left her kids alone while she was at work. The kids got taken to *foster care,* and our neighbor sees them only on weekends.

Mamá and Papi had taught us to say they were in the shower or napping if anyone asked where they were—so no one would know how much they were gone. I could see trouble ahead. Miss would probably think Papi was the cleanest, most well-rested man in Maplewood.

I folded my arms. "Why does Rosa need a swim-suit? You aren't *her* Amiga."

"She could still come with us."

The green beast poked me with one thick claw. I imagined Rosa with my Miss at the mall, laughing and talking. Miss holding Rosa's hand the way she held mine — with Rosa's pinkie wrapped around Miss's pointer finger.

I reached for my hair and started twisting. "Sorry, Miss. Rosa will be gone all day."

12

MISS PROBABLY THOUGHT I'd pick going to the movies for my birthday. But when she asked how I wanted to celebrate, I said, "Can we go to your house?"

Her eyes went wide in surprise. Then she sighed. "Fine."

On the day of my birthday, I got to sit in the front seat of the van because I'd turned twelve. My heart danced in my chest, all the way up a hill, past huge houses. Then my jaw dropped.

I knew her house would be nice, but I didn't expect it to look like a stone castle. I imagined Tinker Bell flying out of the sky and fireworks going off.

Like in the beginning of kids' movies.

She pushed a button on her car's sun visor, and the garage door opened.

Magic.

"Miss, can I push the button next time?"

"Next time?"

I didn't exactly feel welcome. Miss had allowed me to cross *la línea*—the line into the private part of her life. But she wasn't planning to let me stay.

Inside, light came from windows in the ceiling. *What would it be like to live with so much light?* More windows looked onto the backyard. I never knew a family with a backyard to themselves.

Our "garden-level apartment" was just a basement.

Miss glanced around, her face growing red. In three steps she reached a window and slid it open sideways. *A door to the backyard!*

"Guys, get in here."

I heard her boys laughing. Ethan bounded in, like a big shaggy dog. "Hi, J.J."

He meant me—Jacinta Juárez! I'd never had a nickname before.

"You wanna play in the hammock?" he asked.

I didn't know what he meant. I'd never heard of a hammock, but I didn't want him to laugh at me again. Fortunately Miss interrupted.

"Ethan, what are you supposed to be doing?" *Nag-O-Matic.*

He rolled his eyes. Cody followed him into the kitchen, where they started loading the dishwasher.

Miss nodded. "Your psychic powers are truly remarkable."

Our family never used the dishwashers in our apartments, even though Rosa and I begged Mamá to try it. She said people who wouldn't wash a dish were lazy.

I went to join the boys in the kitchen.

I stopped.

A cake with colored sprinkles. Curly letters spelled *Happy Birthday Jacinta* in pink icing. "You made this for me?"

She snorted. "If *I'd* made it, it'd be inedible. Cody's the chef."

I stared at him. *Cooking and cleaning?* I'd never thought of marrying a white boy. Maybe it wasn't a bad idea.

But if Cody was in love with me, it didn't show on his pale little face. He shrugged. "It's from a mix."

"Let the guys work, Jacinta." Miss led me through the glass door to the backyard. "Explain again why Rosa didn't come."

I was irritated that Miss kept asking. It was *my* birthday. Miss was *my* Amiga. So the truth slipped out. I kinda let it slip. "Papi saw her making out."

Miss stopped halfway across the covered patio. "With a *boy*?"

"He touched her"—I stopped, but it was too late—"T-shirt."

Miss's lips pressed together. I got mad at myself for telling on Rosa, but I was also glad, because Miss would know that *I* was the good one.

Then I forgot about Rosa. I was too busy staring. Miss's yard looked like someone had dumped a truckload of flower seeds, then left them where they fell.

"I love the pink ones! How did you plant so many?"

"I didn't. We can't afford a gardener anymore, so the Mexican primroses are taking over."

"You don't like them?"

She studied my face, then smiled. "Actually, I do. They can survive anything. The others are too much trouble."

"Why don't you pull them out?"

She shrugged. "Once you take on something, you feel obligated."

A thought came to me. If I'd known the word, I'd have said it was a *premonition*. A hint of a time when I might be too much trouble, and Miss would still feel *obligated*.

Then she said, "The only flowers worth the time are roses."

Roses? I thought of my sister Rosa. The green beast hissed. "*I'm* named after a flower, too."

"I know. I love hyacinths. I have tons of them."

I stopped again. Mamá always said her girls were a flower garden. Suelita's name meant "little lily." I'd seen lilies in church at Easter. But I'd never seen a hyacinth. "Where are they?"

"They're not in bloom right now."

"Can you show me anyway?"

So she showed me the shriveled brown stems.

"Oh."

"I told you, they already bloomed this year."

My chance to see a hyacinth. And I was late.

Miss went to take a shower, saying she needed to get the TV makeup off her face or she'd break out like Mount Vesuvius.

The boys joined me in the backyard. Ethan ran to get into the hammock, stretched between two trees. *Oh!* A *hamaca*. Abuelita had one on her veranda in Mexico, where I used to take my naps as a little kid. I didn't understand how you could play in one. But that was before I'd met the Dahl boys.

"Let J.J. go first," said Cody. "It's her birthday."

So Ethan got out, and I climbed in. He said, "Grab the sides and wrap it around you. Cover your face."

Cover my face? I got *suspicious.* But I did it.

They started pushing, and the hammock started swinging. My stomach did a flip. I screamed, then laughed.

"Hang on!" shouted Cody.

I rose and fell, my stomach never catching up to

the rest of me. I felt the leaves of the trees brushing the sides of the hammock. I laughed so hard, I couldn't breathe. Then I was upside down! The boys kept pushing. I kept swinging around and around and upside down.

It was probably the most fun I ever had.

I helped Ethan set the table while Cody took the *lasagna* out of the oven. I wished my family could eat together every night, but with Papi working two jobs and Mamá in Mexico, most nights it was just me and my sisters. I felt a lump in my throat as I thought of my last birthday, when Mamá made tamales.

Then I remembered my news. "Miss, I forgot to tell you! I can take gymnastics!"

She looked up from the milk she'd poured. "You have the application?"

"At home."

She went back to pouring. "It's too late for summer gymnastics. You'll have to wait until fall. We need to work on your memory."

Nothing was wrong with my memory. Every day I'd begged Papi to sign the paper. He agreed the day before, when he'd asked what I wanted for my birthday.

I'd said, "The only thing I want is to take gymnastics."

I've said many stupid things in my life, but if I could take back only one, that would be the one. I wish I'd said, "I want our family to be together," and hugged him tight.

Instead I folded my arms and waited.

Papi looked at me. Then he got up and shuffled through the papers by the phone. From his shirt pocket he pulled out a pen and started answering the questions on the scholarship form. When he got to the place for an address, he left it blank. So the people from the city wouldn't know where we lived. So we'd be safe.

Papi was careful. But he wanted me to be happy on my birthday.

Right now—wherever he is—I want him to be happy.

* * *

After dinner Ethan started to put in a movie.

"Miss, I should go home." I'd told Rosa I'd be back early.

"You sure?" Ethan flipped the cover of the movie at me.

I forgot all about my promise to Rosa. This was one movie I hadn't seen. At church they said it was bad. So I *had* to see it. And I kept waiting for the bad parts.

After it was over, I asked Miss, "Why do people think that movie is bad? The boy saved everybody."

"Because there's magic in it." Then she looked concerned. "Will your parents be upset that you watched it?"

"No, Miss. They know magic isn't real."

"Then don't worry about other people. What do *you* think?"

"I loved it!"

"The book is better," said Ethan.

The boy in the movie walked through a brick wall to enter a magical world. I didn't know it, but I was going to do the same thing—cross into an enchanted land just by saying the magic words "I want to read that book."

But right then it was time to go home. When we got to our apartment, Miss came inside to get the paper for the gymnastics class. Suelita must've been in bed, but Rosa stared at the TV, her face frozen. "Mamá said to tell you happy birthday."

My heart slid into my stomach. *"She called?"*

"It's your birthday."

Then I saw the *other* cake. The one Rosa made. My stomach—with my heart still inside—went into a knot.

Mamá walked all the way into town to call and wish me happy birthday. How long had Papi waited before leaving for his night job? Suelita probably cried herself to sleep because she didn't get any cake.

Miss looked at my presents, unopened on the table. She frowned. "You're celebrating tonight? Isn't it rather late?"

I said nothing. Rosa said nothing.

I got the gymnastics paper from the stack by the phone. I handed it to Miss, as the fun of being at her house dissolved like sidewalk chalk in the rain.

"Happy birthday," she said, waiting for me to thank her.

I wanted to. If I hoped to visit her again, I needed to be *gracious*. But I was afraid I would cry. She drifted toward the door, her face confused. My chance was slipping away. "Miss!"

A smile lit up her eyes.

I whispered, "Thanks, Miss. Can I come to your house again?"

She blinked. "We'll see."

Then I was looking at the empty doorway.

LATE ON A FRIDAY NIGHT, my sisters and I played Lotería at Tía's house. It's a Mexican game, kinda like Bingo. It was fun at first.

Suelita kept shouting *"¡Buena!"* whether she'd won or not. Then our cousins did it, too. Standing on kitchen chairs in their diapers with their tiny hands raised to the ceiling.

"¡Buena!"

Tía Carmen, Rosa, and I couldn't stop laughing, but Victor scowled. He kept drinking, getting madder. Tía said we should stop because the babies were sleepy, but Victor insisted we keep playing, swearing at us in Spanish. He didn't like to lose.

I hadn't won a game either, but I didn't care so much. Then, in the last game, I only needed *La Muerte*—the Death card—to win. When Tía flipped over the picture of the skeleton, I raised my arms in triumph. *"¡Buena!"*

Victor stood, his chair crashing into the kitchen wall, and swept the cards to the floor. The babies screamed. Tía ducked. Rosa flinched.

I jumped up, facing Victor, staring into the jagged scar on his eyelid. Whatever happened, I wanted to see it coming.

Victor kicked the table leg. Drinking glasses toppled. Fizzy brown soda spilled across the table, soaking the cards. Victor stormed out, slamming the front door. I started breathing again. We heard tires squealing as his truck roared down the street.

My sisters and I spent the night at Tía's. We sometimes stayed there just for fun—but that night Rosa and I didn't want to leave her alone in case Victor came back. We didn't sleep. We held our aunt's hands and cried together.

When we got home the next day, Rosa and I lied to Papi. We told him our eyes were red from staying up all night, playing Lotería. We didn't want him to forbid us from going to Tía's. But our silence was tinged with black and red—guilt and danger.

We spent the morning napping and watching television. I even told Miss no when she invited us swimming. I was that tired.

Our stories—the ones Miss called Mexican soap operas—had just come on the television when Angélica's number flashed up on caller ID. Rosa waved at me to pick up the phone so the ringing would stop.

"*¿Bueno?*" I heard crying. "Angélica?"

"*Mi papá!*" she sobbed.

My heart came into my throat. "I'm coming right now."

I hung up and turned to Rosa. "I think Angélica's dad got deported."

Rosa pulled her eyes off the television and stared at me. We thought having a parent be deported was the worst thing that could happen to a kid.

We were wrong.

Walking to her apartment, I practiced what I would say. *He'll come back. They always come back.* I rounded the corner and saw neighbors crowding the sidewalk. Angélica's *mamá* sprawled on the grass. Angélica and her little brothers were piled around her, crying.

Torn plastic yellow streamers fluttered from the handrails on the porch. Black writing spelled out the words CRIME SCENE — DO NOT CROSS.

Angélica's *papá* would never come back. Her *papá* was dead.

The next day after church, I sat with Miss in her van in front of our apartment. Her arms remained folded across her chest, waiting for me to talk. My face was swollen from crying, so I had to tell. Not everything. Just the part about Angélica's father.

Then I glanced up. Her eyes tried to see into me, so I lowered my head again.

She unfolded her arms. Her voice was soft. "Please tell your friend I'm so sorry."

I nodded.

"The truck drove up onto the porch?" Miss asked.

I nodded again.

Miss swallowed. "I heard about that. I just didn't realize it happened in your neighborhood. I hope they throw the book at that drunk driver."

She moved one hand to the ignition and the other to the steering wheel.

"They're deporting him," I said. Then I stared at my hands so she wouldn't see my secret.

She froze. "Without a trial?"

Maybe *deported* wasn't the right word. They gave him a choice. Mexico or jail. But I didn't want Miss to think I knew too much, so I nodded as I looped my hair around a finger.

She frowned. "You'd think they'd want him to do some jail time."

Nobody cares if Mexicans kill each other. I didn't say it out loud. But I thought it really hard.

The drunk driver—the one who killed Angélica's father—was Victor. Police said if he came back to America, they'd put him in jail for good. Either way, Tía would be raising their children alone.

I'd sat on the curb and held Angélica. We'd cried together. At the time I didn't know it was Victor who took her *papá* from her. It was good I didn't know. She might've smelled the guilt in me.

But when I got home, I saw Rosa's note. She'd taken Suelita and gone to comfort Tía.

I never liked Victor, but he was part of us.

One more secret for my family to keep.

MAYBE YOU'D THINK I'd feel bad getting bawled out by Miss. Who likes getting yelled at? But Miss was treating me like one of her own kids.

That made me feel good.

And it was better than being at home with Rosa. She was spending the summer watching our cousins so Tía could work. If I'd been there, I'd be taking care of babies, too.

Instead I played in the hammock with the Dahl boys. The three of us landed ourselves in trouble because of Ethan's new game—Kill the Cow. I say *landed* in trouble because I was *airborne* before I hit a sprinkler head. It'd cracked in two.

In this new game, the person who was the "cow" stood in front of the hammock while it swung high and fast with another person inside it. The hammock hit the cow, sending it flying across the yard.

When the sprinkler broke, I was the cow.

Ethan and I agreed to hide the broken piece.

Cody confessed.

Maybe Miss will be glad that I wasn't hurt and forget about the sprinkler. Wrong.

She pressed her lips together. Whiffs of air blew out of her nose, but she wasn't laughing. "The three of you owe me an hour of yard work."

Ethan groaned.

"Each."

At first all three of us worked in the backyard, but Ethan kept snapping at Cody like an angry dog. So Miss put Ethan to work in the front yard. Then it was just Cody and me.

I clipped the shriveled stalks. "Hyacinths are ugly."

Cody smirked. "When you see hyacinths, spring is here. They're dependable."

I'd rather be named for a beautiful flower, but Cody approved of dependability.

"What flower does your mom like best?" I asked *casually*. As though the answer weren't important.

"Roses."

I knew it.

"Cody, are you jealous?" The words popped out before I thought about them.

"Of what?"

"Of—having to share your mom with me?"

He shrugged. "You and the rest of the world."

Maybe having a famous mom wasn't so great.

After an hour we'd filled two trash bags with weeds and clippings. Cody started cutting flowers and putting them in a pail.

"What're you doing?"

"These are for you."

"For me?" My face got hot again.

"Mom told me to."

Oh. I felt like a balloon after someone let the air out. Getting my first flowers from a boy because his mom told him to.

I stood in the kitchen as Miss put my flowers

into a jar. Their smell reminded me of Mamá. I wished I could give them to her. Or to Abuelita. Then I thought, *Mamá and Abuelita have each other. Who do I have?*

Miss hummed while she arranged the flowers. She wasn't wearing her TV makeup, and it made her look both older and younger somehow. Her hair was messy, pulled back in a ponytail. One copper curl fell against her cheek.

"Miss, gardening isn't a good punishment. I like it. Can I work in the garden with *you* sometime?"

She smiled. A new smile. Small and soft. I thought she might say something about spending time with me. Instead she said, "It wasn't punishment. It was your opportunity to fix things. If you break something, you're obligated, right?"

I thought of my picture frame—the one she'd ruined—and nodded. "Right."

"SEE, MISS? It says we owe a lot of money."

She took the letter from my shaking hand.

The envelope said CITY OF MAPLEWOOD. I knew it would be about gymnastics, so I'd opened it, even though it was addressed to Papi. But I was afraid to show it to him.

Dear Mr. Juárez,

The CITY OF MAPLEWOOD is in receipt of your application for recreation scholarships. We are pleased to grant you a discount on the following requested items:

Girls gymnastics class	$35 (with discount) (regularly $55)
Family annual recreation center pass	$355 (with discount) (regularly $925)
Amount due	$390 TOTAL

To take advantage of these scholarships, your family is required to purchase recreation identification cards, $5 per person. Please use this letter when registering.

Sincerely,

Gerald Benton

Gerald Benton
Communications Specialist III

I was glad that my sisters were at Tía's when Miss arrived. I needed her to tell me what to do. Looking back, the answer was simple. I should've thrown the letter away.

"Miss, how'd they know our address?"

She glanced over the top of the letter. "It was on the application." Then her face went all weird. "The address line was blank, so I filled it in. Your dad didn't do that on purpose, did he?"

I wrapped a lock of hair around a finger. "No. He probably just forgot."

Miss look relieved. "That's what I figured."

She took her cell phone from her purse and punched in the number at the bottom of the letter. "Good afternoon, Mr. Benton. This is Kathryn Dawson Dahl."

Miss used her whole name. I smirked. *Leverage.*

"Well, thank you, but I'm hoping to get back to anchoring. Until then, I'm mentoring one of the daughters of the Juárez family. They submitted an application for scholarships?"

Pause.

"They got the letter, but there's no way they can pay for all of this. What about just the gymnastics class?"

I heard a man's voice rumbling.

"Sure, but based on their income, I hoped you'd drop the charge."

Her face froze and she turned away from me.

"You can't assume that. The girls were born in

Colorado." I tried to imagine what Mr. Benton was saying. I walked around Miss so I could read her face, but she turned away again.

"The parents' status has nothing to do with it. The family pays sales tax, so they contribute to your budget, but they're not receiving services."

"Miss—?" I chased her in circles, trying to tell her to forget it.

"I'd like to speak with your supervisor."

Sharp words came through the phone line. Laser beams shot out of Miss's eyes. If Mr. Benton had seen them, his words would've jumped back down his throat. "No, that's not the end of it. Believe me, Mr. Benton, this is *not* the end of it."

Irritated, she punched a button on the phone, then stared at the wall. Her laser-beam eyes looked like they'd burn a hole right through it. So I was surprised when she spoke. Her voice wasn't angry. It was *thoughtful.*

"Jacinta, it's none of my business, but I don't want to start something I can't finish. Do your parents have documentation?"

An earthquake rocked my world.

Never, ever, had anyone asked me that. Even other Mexicans didn't ask.

Miss didn't know that she'd stepped *way* over *la línea*. Much too *personal*.

I didn't want to answer her. I needed time to *think*. My hand found my hair and began twisting. "Of course my parents have papers."

Miss nodded. "That makes things simpler." She started punching buttons on her phone. "Maplewood, Colorado. City manager's office."

At her last three words, my knees turned all watery. I waited until we were in the van before asking. "That lady you called—was that Mr. Benton's boss?"

"His boss's boss."

A trickle of sweat tickled my side. "Is Mr. Benton in trouble?" What I meant was, *Am I in trouble?*

She made her most *dignified* snort. "That would be a yes."

I waited in the chilly gymnastics room for the instructor. Hunched on a mat, with my Michener

Mountaineers T-shirt pulled over my knees, I tried to keep warm.

The temperature wasn't the only reason I was trembling. Blond girls with ponytails bounced around me like popcorn on a stove. Miss *beamed* from the bleachers, but I didn't smile back. *Why did I want this?*

With a splat, then another splat, two girls landed on the mat. One on each side of me.

"Are you in the beginner class, too?" asked the girl with freckles and skinny brown braids.

I looked from her to the other girl. Her hair was frizzy and yellow. Her eyes bulged in a cute-but-ugly way. They both grinned. I wasn't sure what to do. But Cody and Ethan were white, and they were nice. I forced myself to smile and nod.

"It's my third time," said the freckled girl.

"Your third time? In the *beginner* class?"

As soon as they hit the air, I knew they were the wrong words. She looked at the ceiling so the water pooling in her eyes wouldn't roll down her face. "I'm never gonna be good at gymnastics."

Careful to keep my voice gentle, I asked, "Why do you keep taking it if it makes you sad?"

"My mom thinks I'm fat."

I felt the ache in her throat. Like it was my own.

The other girl rolled her bug eyes. "Your mom's anorexic. My mom says I'm clumsy. This is supposed to make me graceful."

I felt sorry for them. *Mamá would never call me fat or clumsy.* Then I remembered my *mamá* wasn't around to call me anything at all.

"Why'd your mom bring you?" asked the girl with the bug eyes.

My stomach lurched. I glanced into the stands at Miss. She smiled and waved. The other girls' eyes followed my look.

The girl with braids said, "Is *that* your mom? Isn't she on the news?"

My hand went right to my hair, my finger twisting and pulling. Like I was trying to yank it all out. Then I nodded.

The bug-eyed girl said, "She's pretty. Come on. Let's jump in the tumbling pit."

* * *

That night—like so many others—I lay awake, counting my lies. Each lie was a little thing. Like a toothpick. A *tower* of toothpicks I kept building taller. One more toothpick, and the whole thing might collapse.

I'd lied saying that Miss was my mom. I'd lied to keep Miss from taking Rosa swimming with us, and I kept lying so Miss wouldn't know Papi had to work all the time. Then there was the big lie, the one that felt the most dangerous—the one about my parents having papers.

And because I'd told so many lies, I had to lie to *myself.*

I told myself everything would be all right.

MISS WAS ANNOYED that I wasn't ready when she got to our apartment. But we were the last ones to arrive at the youth center's Back-to-School Night for kids in the Amigo-Amiga program, so I was happy about the way it turned out. Miss had to park a few blocks away. No one saw her wheezy brown van.

I'd told Angélica she drove a red convertible.

The parking lot was crammed with food booths and a bouncing castle. It was my first time at Back-to-School Night. Angélica had bragged about how much fun she'd had with her Amiga for the past three years.

Now that *I* had an Amiga, it was my chance to get even.

People stared at Miss. Even if you didn't know who she was, with her sunglasses and her hair glowing in the afternoon light, you'd guess she was a TV star.

I slipped my arm through hers. *My* Amiga. She looked at me and smiled. I saw myself grinning back in the twin reflections of her dark lenses.

Mrs. E. stood at the registration table. "Kate!" Her eyes flicked over to me, then back to Miss. "Have you—?"

From the corner of my eye, I caught the tiniest movement of Miss's head. I turned to look at her, but couldn't see past her sunglasses.

I was *uneasy.*

Miss put her hand on my back. "We need to get Jacinta set up for seventh grade."

Mrs. E. reached into a stack behind her and grabbed two backpacks. "Green or purple?"

"Can I get a pink one?"

"Those are for elementary school."

Green or purple—not much of a choice. Purple

is pretty, but it's too sad. I don't want to carry sorrow around all year. But there's already too much jealousy in my life. And green is an ugly color.

"Purple."

"Can we get one for Rosa?" Miss asked.

I stiffened.

Mrs. E. shook her head as she handed me the backpack. "Not until she's in the program."

Until? I whipped my head around to look at Miss.

"Let's get a hot dog." She steered me to the food line. They had cotton candy, but I knew better than to ask Miss for "sugar" before having something *substantial.* We got hot dogs and sodas and sat down.

I had trouble with the ketchup. "Miss, can you open this?"

She took the packet from me and tried tearing at the corner, like it said.

Nothing.

She tried again.

It exploded.

She wiped her face with her hand, leaving a

tomatoey smear across her cheek, then stared at the red stain on her silk blouse.

I got busy eating so she wouldn't see my eyes laughing. I looked to see if Angélica was watching. She wasn't.

She huddled next to her Amiga at a table by themselves. Angélica's eyes were red. Her Amiga rocked her, not saying anything.

Miss hadn't held me like that since the day we met. The green beast whimpered in my belly. But watching Angélica, I knew I didn't have to try to be better than her anymore. With her *papá* dead, she'd always be jealous of me.

The bite of hot dog stayed in my mouth. My jaw refused to chew. I swallowed the piece whole. It ripped my throat all the way down.

I'd seen Angélica at school, but I didn't hang out with her, afraid she'd see the guilt in me.

When Tía was in high school, she used to baby-sit Angélica and her brothers, but Angélica's family had never met Victor. I worried someone would say something—that my guilty secret would come out. In the barrio, you didn't know everyone, but you always knew people who knew other people.

But I was Angélica's best friend. And because of Victor, I owed her. If I hadn't won that last Lotería game, maybe her *papá* would still be alive.

I looked around for something to push Angélica out of my mind. My eyes wandered to the words on the tired brown building—MAPLEWOOD YOUTH RESCUE CENTER. "Miss, what are you rescuing me from?"

She'd poured some of her diet lemon-lime soda on a napkin and was dabbing at the ketchup stain. She looked up. Her eyes followed mine to the sign. "What do *you* think?"

I squinted at the sign and thought of the last few months. Aching for Mamá's arms, Papi working all the time. Feeling *vulnerable*. Worrying about Abuelita. Fighting with a bossy big sister and listening to a whiny little sister who cried aloud for Mamá while I cried in my heart.

The night before Mamá left, alone under the covers with her, I'd accused Mamá of loving Abuelita more than me.

Mamá had stroked my hair. "It's not like that, *mija*. I made Papi come back to America because I wanted our children to get an education. But when we left, Abuelita made me promise that if she ever needed me, I would come back."

I wrapped an arm around her neck. "Then promise you'll come home if *I* ever need you."

She promised. But she'd lied.

And that's when I ran into Miss.

Suddenly my life was full. Going to the movies. Swimming. Gymnastics. Dinners at her big house, swinging in the hammock with Ethan and Cody.

The best was when Miss read to me. She wasn't cuddly. Miss was all knees and elbows. But when she'd read, I'd lean against her, that smell of flowery hair spray. Her words swept me away, to a magic castle where kids flew on broomsticks and fought evil wizards. When Miss stopped reading, I was surprised to be sitting in her family room.

She kept scrubbing at the ketchup stain. The red blob had spread across her chest. Her napkin was shredded, her blouse drenched in lemon-lime soda. And because she was Kathryn Dawson

Dahl, everyone watched. It reminded me of the day we met.

I grinned. "Boredom."

She looked up.

"You rescue me from boredom," I repeated.

The snort.

What I said to Miss was true, but it wasn't the whole truth. In my world, where *family comes first,* Miss saved me from always being last.

We finished our hot dogs. I wanted cotton candy, but as I gathered up my trash, Miss touched my hand. Instantly I missed Mamá. Like she was leaving me all over again. Water came to my eyes.

Miss whispered, "I need to ask you something."

The lump in my throat kept me from answering.

"I'd like to be Rosa's mentor, too."

The green beast stood on its hind legs and roared, breathing fire through my throat, into my head. My eyes burned. "Wha—?"

"I'm worried about Rosa. Her being with that boy."

My face got hot. "I wish I'd never told you that."

"No, it's good you told me, because—"

"Rosa can get her own Amiga!"

Miss squeezed my hand, but I pulled it away.

She sighed. "I can see you're not ready for this."

She sat back and stared at nothing.

The beast settled in my chest.

But he kept one eye open.

AFTER my last *educational opportunity* with Miss—the one where she dragged me to watch a play by *William Shakespeare*—I didn't want to be at home the next time she showed up.

Shakespeare is a dead guy who's *responsible* for the most boring three hours of my entire life. In this play, some lady drops a hanky, gets strangled for it, dies, comes back to life, and tells everybody she killed *herself*—then dies again.

That's the whole show. I'm not even kidding.

And now Miss wanted to take me to the *ballet*? I wasn't even sure what it was. At Halloween, I'd see little girls dressed in pink tights, wearing tiny crowns and scratchy, poofy skirts. Angélica said the ballet was ladies dancing on their tippy-toes to old music, which sounded really stupid.

So when Miss's name flashed up on the phone, I let it ring. Maybe she'd think nobody was home and go to the ballet without me.

Rosa stopped feeding Suelita. "Who is it?"

"Miss."

The phone rang.

"Answer it!"

"I don't want to talk to her."

The phone rang.

Rosa moved to get it.

I snatched it up. *"¿Bueno?"*

"Jacinta? It's Kate. Sometimes it's cold in the theater, so bring a sweater. Not that ratty one. Something nice."

"Miss, I can't go."

Pause. "Because—?"

"I—my dad's at work—we have to watch Suelita."

"Rosa's there?"

Trapped. Rosa glared at me, a spoonful of rice motionless on the way to Suelita's open mouth.

"Yesss."

"Then you can go! Are you dressed?"

"No."

"Get dressed! These tickets are expensive." Miss was always telling me how much things cost. "I'll be there in fifteen minutes."

Click.

It was Rosa's turn to yell. "You can stay with Suelita, fix dinner, and do laundry. *I* will go with Miss!"

"She's *my* Amiga!"

"Not if you won't go with her!"

"I'm going!" I stomped into our bedroom and slammed the door.

I wasn't ready when Miss arrived, so she drove fast — even though she knew it scared me — speeding to "make up some time." She broke the silence. "You look nice."

Since Miss wouldn't let me wear Mamá's sweater to the ballet, I'd had to borrow Rosa's. Crossing my arms, I stared out the window. The Rocky

Mountains towered on the left. I heard Miss's voice in my head. "You'll never get lost if you remember the mountains are west!"

That was the *educational opportunity* when Miss had handed me a map and we drove all over Maplewood. She forced me to give directions. To the store, to the library, to my school. She made me say, *Go south,* or *Turn east,* instead of saying, *Go right,* or *Turn here,* like everyone else does. Always pushing me to learn stupid stuff.

So I was still frowning when she drove into a parking garage. She pulled into a space and switched off the motor. I expected her to sprint across the parking lot like always. Instead she turned to me, her voice tired. "Could you at least *try* to appreciate this educational opportunity?"

Nag-O-Matic.

I stared at the concrete wall in front of us. "I get 'educational opportunities' at school. The Amiga program is supposed to be *fun.*"

"You had fun at the television station. You spent half an hour on the weather computer."

"But that last educational opportunity was *boring*. What kid likes Shakespeare?"

"How many times can I apologize for that?"

"Angélica's Amiga lets her pick where they go."

Her eyebrows came together in the middle. "You want me to be like *other* people?"

My stomach twisted. "Sometimes. When you make me do weird stuff."

One of her eyebrows went up.

"Like *Shakespeare*," I added.

"Some people like *Othello*. It's romantic."

"It's stupid. The choking part was good, but real people don't talk like that."

She sighed. "Your world is too small."

I wasn't really mad at Miss. I'd told myself I was, but it was another lie. I was mad at Mamá. If she'd been home, I wouldn't need some *gringa* who tried to turn me into someone I wasn't. I wouldn't even talk to Mamá the last time she called. But she still hadn't agreed to come back.

Miss hurried me to the back door of a massive stone building and pushed the buzzer. She gave the man her name. Her *names*. All of them.

He led us down a corridor.

"This doesn't look like a theater," I told him.

"We're backstage. I'm taking you to the green room."

"Everything is green? Like the Emerald City?" I thought of the "film classic" that Ethan had made me watch.

The man grinned. "The place performers wait is called the green room, no matter what color it is."

I let out an angry huff. One more person who smiled because I didn't know stuff. But then he opened a door, and I forgot to be annoyed.

Fairies filled the room. Kids smaller than me wearing wings, and ladies dressed like flowers. One man wore a tight costume the color of his skin, like he was naked. Except for a big leaf.

A woman turned. "Kate! I do not see you for a long time!"

On her golden head sat a glittering crown. Sparkles covered her skin. The fairy queen floated across the room to us. Smiling, she gave Miss little air-kisses, one on each cheek.

Miss pulled away from the fairy's clingy skirt, which left bits of glitter on her black velvet pants. "Nadine Robert, meet Jacinta."

The fairy took my hands. *"Enchantée!"*

"Where are you from?" I breathed. Miss smirked. I should've said, *How do you do?*

The fairy smiled. "I am from France."

"Nadine attended the Paris Opera School," said Miss.

"Opera?" Even the word sounded boring.

Nadine Robert smiled again. "Do not worry. We have no opera tonight. Just the ballet. *A Midsummer Night's Dream.* By William Shakespeare."

"*Shakespeare?*" Horrified, I turned to Miss.

She grabbed my shoulders and steered me away. "Uh — Nadine, can we drop by after the show?"

How could she? I'd been learning Miss's words, so I knew what to call it. *Betrayal.* But if I was going to spend the afternoon pouting, this was a good place to do it. Red velvet seats near the stage, and floors that weren't sticky. A chandelier hung from the ceiling.

And there were *three balconies.* I pointed at the seats floating in the air. "Miss, we should sit there next time."

She smirked. "Next time?"

My face got hot. *I won't have a good time, no matter what.*

Miss said, "I usually do sit up there. I can't afford these seats. The youth center got them for us."

Oh.

"That's why I'd like to be Rosa's mentor, too. We could all get free tickets."

I folded my arms again. To help me remember *not* to have a good time.

The lights dimmed. In the darkness, music started. I hung on to the armrests, my fingernails digging into the plush velvet. But the music reached out and swept me away. I've never seen the ocean, but it'd be like this. Waves of music flowed through me and into me.

I tried — really, really hard — to *hate* the ballet.

But it's hard not to laugh when couples chase each other through a magical forest where fairies fly around making everybody fall in love with the wrong person. And it's very, *very* hard not to like a show when Nadine Robert—the most beautiful woman in the world—is in love with a guy who has the head of a donkey.

Backstage, Nadine Robert signed my program. Her last name was spelled like the boy's name, and not the way it sounded: row-BEAR.

Next to her picture she wrote, *Pour ma chère amie Jacinta*. Miss said it was French—"For my dear friend Jacinta."

The same thing Eva Chávez had written.

"How many famous people do you know, Miss?"

She snorted. "Not nearly enough."

I wished that Mamá could see the ballet. She liked beautiful things.

Why am I thinking about her? She's not thinking about me. I shoved her image out of my mind.

Back in the van, Miss said, "Keep that program. Nadine Robert is a true artist."

That's when I knew "art" isn't just things in a museum. Art can be fleeting *and* eternal. I thought that up myself. It sounded like poetry, so I said it over and over in my mind.

Fleeting and *eternal*.

Like something Nadine might say in her low, throaty voice. Without thinking, I said, "I'd like to talk French."

18

I WIPED my sweaty hands on the van seat when Miss drove past the sign: MAPLEWOOD COMMUNITY COLLEGE. *Why did I let her talk me into this? A French class? With grown-ups? What kid in seventh grade wants to spend more time in school?*

Maybe you'd think I should've learned to trust Miss, but she kept pushing me to try stuff that was harder and harder. She'd reminded me that learning French was *my* idea in the first place. I was flattered that she thought I could do this.

And maybe some part of me wondered if I could.

Miss shut off the van and jumped out, striding across the dark parking lot. I followed slowly, dragging my feet.

I couldn't talk to Angélica about it. I still avoided her, afraid I'd blurt out the story of how I beat Victor at Lotería the night he killed her *papá.* A black cloud of guilt surrounded me. A *double* black cloud, because I knew Angélica needed me.

Avoiding her was easy, now that we didn't have the same classes.

When school had started, Miss made sure I was "properly assessed"—which made Mamá happy when I told her. All her dreams for me were coming true.

I liked my smart-kid classes okay. Everybody was nice, but smart kids think mostly about school and grades. They don't know what it's like to miss their *mamás* or worry about their *papás* getting killed or deported. Without Angélica, I didn't have anyone who knew the *whole* me.

Miss was an earthquake, splitting my world in two while I straddled the crack that grew wider. A new life beckoned on one side. My old life called from the other. If I didn't pick a side soon, I'd fall into the *chasm* in the middle, and no one would see me again.

Miss continued her long strides across the parking lot, assuming I was scampering behind her like a trained dog. *When's she going to notice that I'm not with her? If she has to walk back for me, will she decide I'm too much trouble? Will she just drive me home? Then what?*

Rosa would've been happy to trade places with me. I'd lied to her—saying I was going to the Dahls' for dinner—afraid she'd tell Papi about the French lessons.

If Mamá had been home, she could've made Papi understand that learning new things is good. But without Mamá to explain, I didn't know what Papi would do if he discovered I was taking a college class.

Sighing, I raced after Miss. By the time I caught up with her, I was puffing. "You walk too fast."

"We wouldn't be rushing if you'd been ready. Where's your watch?"

Miss bought it for me because I was late all the time, but until that moment I hadn't thought of it as a *tool.* I wore it to school to show my friends, then left it in my jewelry box.

"Je m'excuse." I apologized in French, knowing it would make her forget being *exasperated*.

"Allons-y," she said. It means, "Let's go."

"This is a college?" It looked like a middle school. Only bigger.

"Bien sûr," she said, which means "of course." "Community college. You'll go here after high school."

College. Miss said I'd be going to college.

Just. Like. That.

My teachers talked about college, and I'd assumed they were talking to the American kids. But when Miss said it, she was talking to *me*. I thought a moment. "I don't want to go to this college."

She stopped on the concrete steps. She turned, her eyes hard, ready for a fight. Before she could speak, I blurted, "I want to go to Michener University."

Someone should've been there with a video camera. Someone could've made ten thousand dollars on that TV show for the funniest home movie. For one moment, her icy look was frozen. Then it melted. She collapsed on the stairs, laughing. Not her airy snort. A laugh that echoed off the building and filled the whole night sky.

I sat on the step next to her, and she pulled me close. She gasped out, "You never cease to surprise me!"

So *I* started giggling. Then Miss's laugh exploded again. And that made me laugh even harder.

I don't know what was so funny. But every time we tried to stop, one of us would snort, and we'd crack up again. Tears streamed into our open mouths. People hurrying up the steps stared at us, smiling, wishing they were part of the joke. I clung to Miss. My sides hurt, but I didn't care. I wanted to sit in the dark with her and laugh forever.

Miss opened the classroom door and glanced at the clock. We were two minutes late, but she didn't *spontaneously combust,* as Ethan always predicted.

I didn't know whether to be relieved or disappointed.

Miss put her hand on my back and guided me to a desk right in front, even though the rest of the class members lined the walls.

The teacher's thick glasses made his eyes tiny and far away. His soul seemed to be in a different galaxy. That first night, Monsieur Visser *talked about* speaking French more than he actually spoke French. Mostly he talked about living in Amsterdam during the Nazi occupation.

In the car on the way home, I asked, "Isn't Amsterdam where Anne Frank lived?"

Miss glanced at me, impressed that I knew about the Jewish girl who lived in hiding during World War II.

"We're reading about her in school," I explained.

"You like your classes?"

"I like Language Arts." It's easy to like stuff you're good at. And suddenly, I was good at Language Arts.

The teacher was the same one I'd had last year. Mr. Flores had asked me to read aloud the first day. I picked up the book, thinking about the summer days when Miss read to me. Afternoons when her words flowed like music.

In the classroom, the words flowed out of *me*. Mr. Flores stopped me. "You've been reading over the summer?"

I nodded. "With my mentor."

I would've felt silly calling Miss my Amiga to Mr. Flores. I didn't think he'd understand. He gave a slight shake of his head. "Thank your mentor."

And for the first time *I* understood. *Mentor.* Not just an *amiga*. Not even a tutor. Miss was more. She was showing me that I could decide who I wanted to be.

When Miss's van pulled up to our apartment, Rosa and Tía Carmen were sitting on the steps, watching Suelita and my cousins play on the grass in the cool darkness. Before I got out of the van, Rosa ran up to Miss's window.

"What did Cody make for dinner?" Like me, she was amazed that a boy could cook.

Miss frowned. "Dinner? Jacinta and I are taking French at the community college."

I almost choked on my own spit. Rosa looked across the van at me. Using just my eyes, I pleaded with her not to say anything. After a million years, Rosa nodded. "That's nice, Miss."

Then Rosa said, "Jacinta, it's your turn to wash

dishes. But first give Suelita a bath and put her to bed."

I was Rosa's slave.

Anything she wanted me to do, I had to do, or she'd tell Papi I was taking a college class. Dishes, laundry, babysitting Suelita. Rosa would lie on the sofa and order me to bring her a drink. I'd carry the glass thinking, *I should dump this on your stupid head!*

But *I* was stupid for letting Rosa get away with it. I should've told Miss I didn't want to take French, especially since part of me didn't.

But part of me did.

It's easy to like what you're good at — and I was good at French. Better than the grown-ups in class. Better than Miss.

"Jacinta!"

I stopped and looked around. Angélica's Amiga followed me out of the school. Her glasses bounced on their chain as she jogged up to me. Taking me by my arms, she peered into my face. "Have you seen Angélica?"

I inhaled her baby-powder smell. "No, Miss Linda."

"The school says she hasn't been here for two weeks."

My best friend? I didn't notice she was missing? Black and purple waves of guilt and sorrow washed over me.

Her voice broke. "I bought her that phone so this wouldn't happen. Do you know where they might've gone?"

Her words clanked in my hollow insides. "I'm sorry, Miss."

"Can I give you my phone number? In case she calls you?"

I thought about telling her that this is how it works in the barrio. Once when Papi got sick for a few weeks, he lost his job. He got a new job when he got better, but by then we were too far behind in our rent to ever catch up. We had to move. In the night. Without telling anyone.

But Miss Linda rummaged through the wadded

tissues in her purse for a pen. She looked at me, her red eyes swimming.

I held out my palm. "Sure, Miss. Write your phone number on my hand, so I won't lose it."

I didn't wash that hand for three days.

Then I saw the garbage bin outside Angélica's building. While workmen dragged the family's stuff out of their apartment, neighbors picked through the open container, like crows on a dead squirrel.

I ran home and took a shower. *I'm glad Papi has two jobs now. That could never happen to us again.*

I scrubbed the ink off my hand.

During French classes, three young women with British accents sat in the back of the room giggling. Mr. V. never seemed to hear them.

Miss was *beyond* irritated.

"Just tell them to leave!" she told Monsieur Visser one day after class.

He seemed to shrink in front of her. "Programs that don't meet the minimum enrollment get canceled. I depend on foreign students to register, whether they care about the class or not."

It made no sense. I asked, "Why do they sign up, if they don't want to learn French?"

Mr. V. peered at me with his tiny eyes. "They have to take one class each semester to stay in the United States on educational visas."

They can stay in America by being rude in French class? My gut twisted as I thought of the scars on Mamá's arms, of what she'd face to get back home.

I wanted to throw up.

I snatched up the phone on the first ring.

Mamá always called just before Papi left for his night job, but that day Papi had needed gas for his truck, so he'd left early. I put Mamá on speaker-phone so Rosa and I could both hear. We leaned in, hungry for her sound of her voice. Suelita slept next to us on the sofa, so we talked softly.

"When are you coming home?" The same question I always asked.

Mamá voice was raspy, "Abuelita is worse, *mija*. I need to stay until—as long as she needs me."

Until? Until what? Abuelita is going to die?

I didn't ask the question out loud. Neither did Rosa.

Mamá asked, "How are your studies?"

I was distracted, worried about Abuelita, so words just fell out. "Miss and I are taking French at—at the community college."

Rosa and I stared at each other. I held my breath. *Why don't I think before I open my mouth?*

Mamá's voice was full of surprise. "That is wonderful, *mija*. Papi is not worried?"

What's wrong with me? One minute I can't shut up. The next, I can't speak!

"He says it is okay," Rosa lied. Then she reached across the sofa to gently shake our little sister. "Mamá, Suelita is waking up. She wants to talk to you."

After we hung up the phone, Rosa and I washed the dishes.

Together.

"YOU ARE BRAVE," said Rosa.

I looked up, surprised. We were alone in the rec center locker room. I'd asked Tía to watch Suelita so Rosa could come with Miss and me. I owed my sister for covering for me with Mamá about the French class. But I didn't expect any compliments. "Brave? Me?"

"Taking gymnastics."

"The practice beam is only one foot off the ground!"

"Not that. The white girls. Miss says you made friends on the very first day."

I remembered that class, how scared I was. I raised my eyebrow, giving Rosa the look Miss sometimes gave me. "You talked about me?"

Rosa sighed. "We talked about *me*. Miss says my world is too small. But I am not brave like you."

I opened my mouth, but no sound came out. I tried again, and this time the words came out all by themselves. "Miss wants to be your mentor."

Rosa looked confused. "What about you?"

"She can mentor both of us." I expected Rosa to be excited. Or at least smile. She frowned. *"What?"* I asked.

"Jacinta, I am not brave like you. Miss makes you do things, and you do them."

I didn't know if Rosa was crazy or if I was. She'd spent months being jealous. *Now Rosa doesn't want Miss?* I'd been hogging Miss, keeping her for myself. *Suddenly I want to share?*

Maybe you'd think I was being kind. But you would be wrong. I just didn't want to be in Miss's world alone anymore, especially since Angélica was gone. If Rosa and I were together, there'd be at least one person in the world who understood the *whole* me, not just bits and pieces.

Instead of arguing with Rosa, I talked to Miss later, telling her I was worried about the *boys* hanging around Rosa. Then I told Papi that Rosa needed an Amiga — to keep her out of *trouble.*

Against Papi *and* Miss? Rosa never stood a chance.

I was excited when the youth center got tickets to a *professional* basketball game for kids in the Amigo-Amiga program. When I told Miss that Rosa and I wanted to go, she said basketball wasn't her "thing."

I said, "If *I* can watch all *five* acts of *Othello,* then *you* can watch *one* basketball game."

She got the tickets.

But on the day of the game, nothing went right. Even though I tried to explain to Rosa that a watch is a *tool,* she wasn't ready when Miss arrived. And because Miss is cheap, we had to stop to buy snacks. No way was she going to pay the sports arena food prices.

By the time we got there, a sign said LOT FULL. The youth center had given us a parking pass, but Miss had to *pay* at another lot far away.

We walked back to the arena with Miss's heels making angry clicks on the pavement. We stood in line—something Miss hated. Then we got sent to *another* line for a "security check" because of our purses. Waves of annoyance radiated from Miss. "How long is this going to take?"

"Sorry, ma'am. Just checking for weapons."

But after poking about in her purse, the usher said she couldn't bring her snack into the arena. Miss's face made me take a step back.

She was a tornado. In a whirlwind of elbows, she flipped her purse upside down, dumping out the package of trail mix. It hit the floor and broke open. The crowd mobbing to see the basketball game danced around pieces of dried fruit and nuts skidding across the tiles. The usher groaned.

In a huff, Miss pushed past him. My heart slid up to my throat. Whispers hissed around me.

"Did you just see—?" "Isn't she—? The one on the news?"

Rosa and I hurried after Miss. My sister trembled. "That guard could arrest her! Why did she do that?"

The answer struck me. *Because she can!* Miss had the *luxury* of being able to make a scene— something our parents could never afford.

I knew that Rosa was afraid of the man's uniform. "He's not a guard—just an usher."

Rosa mumbled, "We'll need the *Mentors'* Rescue Center to get her out of jail."

I grinned—until I realized that I was smiling because Rosa didn't know stuff.

Red with embarrassment, Miss waited for us to catch up. "I shouldn't have done that. Do you think anyone recognized me?"

I lied. "No, you're good. And I still have the candy. We can share."

Understanding came into Rosa's face. "I still have the chips! After you threw your stuff, nobody checked me! Did you do that on purpose?"

"No!" After a pause Miss added, "We probably should turn over the rest of the snacks, too."

Puppy-dog eyes. "Please, Miss! We didn't lie. Nobody *asked* if we had any food."

She shook her head. "What kind of example am I setting? You need a different mentor."

I smirked. "No way, Miss!"

*   *   *

Some things make sense. Like French. Maybe it was because I already spoke two languages, but French was easy. What *doesn't* make sense is deporting people who want to work, but welcoming rude girls who sit and yak in the back of a French class.

The three of them gabbed right through Monsieur Visser's explanation of the *passé composé*. I was mad, and didn't consider what Miss or Mr. V. would think. I slapped my pen on my notebook and marched to the back of the room. I stood over those girls with my hands on my hips, *glowering*. I didn't care that they were older than me. I didn't care that they were white. The giggling stopped like I'd yanked out the cord on a television.

After the clock ticked off the longest minute in history, I walked back to my seat. Without saying a word.

The class continued.

I glanced at Miss, afraid of what I'd see. Her eyes were leaking, and she bounced in her chair. Her hand covered her mouth. It seemed like she was trying to swallow her lips.

She's trying not to laugh!

That's when I realized power doesn't come from your job or the color of your skin. Real power comes from inside. It's not something that someone can give you.

And it's not something that anyone can take away.

WE CELEBRATED CHRISTMAS three weeks early at the Dahls'. Ethan and Cody were going to be with their dad over winter break, so Miss was flying to Florida to visit her mother. Miss had vacation time because she'd worked for 5News since "before the invention of dirt."

I was irritated. Mamá never got vacation days. When she went to Mexico, she'd had to quit her job.

If I was being honest, I'd admit I was jealous that Miss could jump on plane to visit her mother, while I hadn't seen Mamá in months. It wasn't fair that some people get everything.

And maybe that's why I picked a fight.

"Your mom owns this house. That means you're *rich*," I insisted.

"We're not rich!" Cody and Ethan said together. Like they'd practiced it.

I looked to Rosa for support. She concentrated on the kernel she'd threaded onto her popcorn chain and wouldn't join the argument. The Dahls' household was new to her.

Ethan said, "We're middle class. *You're* poor. You use the food bank."

"I am never talking to you again, Ethan Dahl!" I shouted.

Miss whisked around the corner, carrying a plate of spicy cookies shaped like little people. *"Ethan."*

"I'm just stating a fact!"

"Enough."

He stomped out of the room. Miss sighed, then looked from Rosa to me. "It's all relative. I'm sure your family in Mexico thinks of you girls as rich Americans."

"We're not Americans," I said.

"You were born in Denver, right?"

"Yes, but—"

"Then you're Americans."

I blurted, "We're *Mexicans*. We're proud to be Mexicans!"

Miss opened her mouth to argue with me, but closed it again when Rosa nodded in agreement.

Rosa and I were both born in Colorado, but our family moved back to Mexico right after I was born. Abuelo had fallen from his horse and hit his head. He couldn't work. Mamá and Papi had to return to help run the farm.

By the time I was six, Abuelo had died, and my *tíos*, Mamá's two younger brothers, were old enough to help. So Mamá told Papi we needed to move back to America, that it was time Rosa and I started school. Mamá would remind us all the time that we were U.S. citizens. But in our hearts, Rosa and I knew we were Mexican.

Moving around the Dahls' fake tree, I searched for the best place to hang the ornament shaped like a nutcracker. I hadn't known what a nutcracker was until Miss took Rosa and me to see that ballet.

Cody had shrugged when I'd asked if he was

jealous that he didn't get to go with us. "It's not my favorite ballet."

It was weird that a boy would have a favorite ballet. Later, I'd wish I'd asked what his favorite was.

Backstage I'd introduced Rosa to Nadine Robert, who played the Sugar Plum Fairy. *"Madame Robert, je vous présente ma sœur."*

Nadine had kissed me on both cheeks and said my French was wonderful.

Miss thought so, too, although she wouldn't speak French with me when other people were around. She said it was rude. But we practiced whenever we were alone.

I gave up looking for an empty spot on the front of the Christmas tree. I moved another decoration from where Cody had hung it so I could put the nutcracker smack in the middle.

Then I looked at what I held in my hand. A picture frame. The writing said *Baby's First Christmas.* An angel peeked lovingly into a *bassinet.* The photo was of a sleeping child. A lump rose in my throat. I glanced around to see if anyone was reading my thoughts.

The baby had creamy skin. Long brown lashes lay across his round pink cheeks. I could tell by the date stamped on the ornament that it was Cody in the picture. We were born the same year. If Miss had been *my* mother, then this picture could be—

No, don't think about that. Mamá's coming home soon. I need to wait for Mamá.

She had finally admitted that Abuelita was dying.

I loved Abuelita. When I was little, she'd hold me on her lap and tickle my tummy. She used to sneak cookies to us before dinner. If Mamá found out, we'd all just laugh.

Since moving to Colorado, we'd only been to visit Abuelita once. Coming back, Rosa and I had to ride *alone* on the bus for more than a day. But it took Mamá weeks to get home. When she finally did return, we saw the evidence of the crossing on her worn and beaten body. Papi forbid us to ever return to Mexico.

"It's too dangerous," he'd said. Abuelita had never even seen Suelita.

But when Abuelita got sick, Papi couldn't stop Mamá from going to her.

Rosa and I still talked about living with our parents on Abuelita's farm when we grew up. A place we could be happy, be together, without ever having to worry about our parents getting deported.

I loved Abuelita. Really.

BUT—if she *had* to die—I hoped she'd die soon.

That's terrible to say. Wrong to even *think*. I *hated* myself for thinking it.

But I needed Mamá to come home. Because sometimes at night, I'd lie awake imagining life in Miss's big house, cooking and gardening with Cody, making movies with Ethan. Cody and I would ride the bus to high school together. Then I'd go to Michener University. When I graduated, I wouldn't be cleaning houses. Someone else would clean *my* house.

The only way for that to happen was if there were no Mamá. No Papi. Mamá needed to come back so I'd stop thinking bad thoughts.

In my hand I still held the sparkling angel frame. I hung it on a branch at the very bottom of the tree. Way in the back.

* * *

After dinner I felt Rosa's eyes on my mouth as I chewed each sticky sweet bite of the pecan pie. She couldn't have any because Miss had taken her to get braces. Nuts weren't allowed.

"Has anyone teased you about your braces?" Miss asked Rosa.

Rosa pulled her eyes off my mouth and focused on her. "Why would they tease me?"

"Kids used to laugh about my braces when I was a teenager. They don't do that anymore?"

"No," said Rosa.

"Yes," said Ethan.

They looked at each other.

"If you have braces, it means you're rich," said Rosa.

Ethan looked at me. "Then your family's rich, and we're not."

"Ethan," Miss warned.

"You're getting braces," Cody said to Ethan.

"When we can afford it," said Miss.

While Ethan made a face at Cody, I asked, "Miss, why didn't you buy Ethan's braces first?"

The word for her look is *dumbfounded.* "I didn't

buy Rosa's braces. There's a program for families without insurance."

"Why don't you take Ethan there?" I asked.

"I make too much money."

"Ha!" I said to Ethan. He made another ugly face.

"Boys, time to do the dishes," said Miss.

They both groaned. Rosa stood. "I'll help."

As they cleared the table, I whispered to Miss, "Are you mad that Rosa gets her braces for free?"

"Why would I be mad?"

"It's unfair. You're an American and you have to pay."

She smirked. "We only *think* we want fairness. We should be asking for *grace*."

I didn't understand. Teachers, parents, and grown-ups all over the world are always telling kids to "play fair." *How can fairness be bad? And grace?* I'd heard of *grace* at church. Miss was always reminding me to be *gracious* when I'd forget to thank her for stuff. I'd thought maybe *grace* meant being polite. But that didn't seem to fit. I asked, "What *is* grace?"

Miss thought. "When you get something wonderful that you don't deserve—a blessing you haven't earned."

Usually she was good at explaining things. But not this time.

"I don't get it."

She patted my arm. "Think about it."

Miss handed a red gift bag to Rosa, but before Rosa could open it, Miss said, "That's for Carmen. For her new baby. What'd she name him?"

"Mateo," said Rosa.

Miss nodded and smiled.

"Can we open it?" I asked.

"No!"

As Miss tore the paper off my present to her, a smile spread across my face. Then she smirked, examining the doll I'd bought at the drugstore. "How nice!"

"I got you a doll because your name is Doll!"

Ethan snickered. "Our name is *Dahl*. D-A-H-L."

I blushed, suddenly remembering all the times I'd seen her name on TV, written underneath her face while she reported the news. *Why hadn't I paid attention?*

"*Guys,*" their mother warned as Cody started giggling. They were laughing because I didn't know something. But it was funny. I giggled, too.

Then Rosa started. And finally Miss.

Many moments later she wiped her eyes. Then she picked up two small boxes made of shiny red foil and tied with green ribbons. She checked the tags and held one out to Rosa and the other to me.

Just as my hand touched the box, I glanced at Miss. Something in her face made me hesitate.

Rosa ripped off the ribbon, opened her box, then pulled out a ring. "Miss!"

As Rosa flew past me to hug Miss, I tore open my own box. Then I paused. In the glow of the Christmas lights, the ruby sparkled. My birthstone. Pink. It meant more than just hope. A promise *fulfilled.* I stared at the ring on its bed of cotton until the image got blurry. *Miss loves me.*

I slipped the ring on. It fit. Like it was made for me.

Miss sent the boys away so we could have *the*

conversation. She explained that she was giving us *purity* rings. By taking them, Rosa and I were promising not to be alone with a boy. Then her face wrinkled up. "Will your parents mind me giving these to you?"

"No, Miss!" Rosa and I answered together, clutching the rings to our chests.

Rosa's ring had an *amethyst* in it. Purple. *For sorrow?* I was glad I got the pink one. With Mamá gone, I needed all the hope I could get.

That night in bed I left the curtain of our window pulled back so I could still admire the ring on my hand in the light from the streetlamp.

Papi had thought the rings were pretty when we showed him, but when Rosa explained that they were "purity rings," he got upset. I didn't understand why. He was as worried as Miss about us getting pregnant—not that he had any reason to worry. But maybe Papi thought Miss had crossed *la línea.* That the gifts were too *personal.* Maybe he thought Miss was acting too much like a *mom.*

And that made *me* angry. *Doesn't every kid*

deserve a mom? Don't I deserve a mom? The word for how I was feeling about Miss is called *defensive.*

At least Papi didn't say anything about making us give the rings back.

I turned my hand back and forth so I could watch the ruby sparkle. I didn't need a purity ring— I didn't know any boys I wanted to be alone with. But the ring meant something different to me than it did to Miss. *A promise that she'll always be there for me.*

A promise my own *mamá* couldn't keep.

I STUMBLED through the dark, tripping over packages and almost knocking down our Christmas tree. I had to reach the phone before it stopped ringing.

Because nobody calls at two in the morning to say hello.

The sharp smell of pine burned my nose, and prickly needles scratched my face as I grabbed the handset. *"¿Bueno?"*

Even while I said the word, I knew that things were not "good." Before she spoke, before I heard Mamá crying, I knew.

Abuelita is dead.

Mamá talked, but I wasn't hearing her. The screaming in my head was too loud. I gave the phone to Rosa without an argument when she put out her hand for it.

Is this my fault? Did I wish Abuelita dead? And part of my brain asked the *other* questions. *Is there time for Mamá to cross the border? Can she be home by Christmas?*

I helped my sister pack the suitcase she had borrowed from Tía. Rosa kept wiping her face on her sleeve. My eyes were dry.

Rosa packed the perfume we bought for Mamá at the drugstore. I added another wrapped package to the suitcase — the sweater Miss bought for me and Suelita to give to Rosa for Christmas. It didn't take a genius to figure out that Miss also got a sweater for my sisters to give to me. I'd already sworn to myself I wouldn't wear it until Mamá came home.

Mamá had said Rosa was old enough to ride the bus to Mexico by herself, so she could attend Abuelita's funeral.

"You love Rosa more than me," I'd accused into the phone.

Mamá said, "You don't want to come to the funeral. Your heart would break, *mija*."

"It's broken already."

"Jacinta, you must stay with Papi. To care for Suelita. And what about Carmen? She needs help with the new baby. With Mateo. They all need you now. *¿Sí?*"

"*Sí.*" The word was sour in my mouth.

"You are almost a woman, *mija*. A woman must be strong. Even more than a man."

Is Mamá stronger than Papi? I thought of how she had pushed him to come to America so that we could get an education. How she had gone to Mexico to care for Abuelita while she was dying, even though Papi said no. *How strong do you have to be to watch your mamá die?*

I thought of how difficult and dangerous it'd be for Mamá to come home.

Then I thought of Tía Carmen raising three children by herself. She could've gone back to Mexico with Victor. But even though she was scared about raising her children alone, Tía wanted education for her children, too.

And I thought of Rosa. She was still a girl, but she'd been there for Suelita, who was a baby when Mamá left. To Suelita, Rosa was more like a mother than a sister.

And Rosa had been there for me.

I'd thought Miss was the most powerful woman I'd ever met, with strength in tones of copper and steely blue. But Miss's strength had never been tested. Her creamy skin wasn't covered in scars. I realized that there are many different shades to being a strong Mexican woman. As many colors as in Abuelita's afghan.

When it was time for Rosa to leave, I stood in front of our building and held Suelita while she whimpered. Snow fell in fat, wet clumps as Rosa climbed into Papi's truck.

Suelita's tiny body shivered, but I felt nothing.

Papi would drive Rosa to the bus station. Then he'd go to the first of his two jobs.

Mamá and Rosa would spend Christmas burying Abuelita.

I would go to Tía's and care for Suelita and my cousins during winter break so Tía could work.

We put aside our grief.

We did what we had to do.

22

I DIDN'T WANT to talk, but Miss didn't care. She wanted answers. "Rosa went on a bus? By herself?"

"*Yessss.* She comes home tonight."

Miss massaged her temples.

The older waitress at Mom's Diner ambled up to our booth. "Whatcha gonna have?"

Miss took her hands away from her face. "Just coffee."

The waitress turned to me. "And what would *you* like?"

She could tell that I'd been crying. By then I knew that waitresses were nice because they'd get bigger tips. I didn't feel *obligated* to be nice in return, but it'd become a habit. I looked into her eyes. "Root beer, please."

I thought about the early days of going to Mom's Diner. Miss was always telling me, "Sit up straight and look the server in the eye. It's rude otherwise. It's like telling people they don't exist."

This lesson had been hard. I wasn't trying to be rude. In Mexico, we lower our eyes as a sign of respect. I'd told this to Miss.

She'd said, "That won't work in the United States. If you want people to trust you, you look them in the eye. Eyes are the window to the soul."

I didn't like the idea of people seeing into my soul. It made me too *vulnerable*. But I'd learned to look the server in the eye.

Once the waitress left, Miss and I had nowhere to look except at each other. We saw the misery in each other's souls. Then we both looked away.

Miss spoke. "What were your parents thinking? You know what it's like in Mexico. Drugs. Kidnappings."

She said other stuff, but I didn't hear it. *Why am I getting a lecture? I've been here washing dishes and changing smelly diapers. Navidad* had always been full of warmth, full of light. This year Christmas had been dark and cold. Empty.

I'd been waiting for Miss to come back from her vacation so there'd be someone to pay attention to *me*. Instead she was worried about Rosa.

By the time we left Mom's Diner, I thought Miss was finally done talking. But after she drove me home, she parked outside our apartment and turned off the engine. Like when Pastor Federico clears his throat before saying someone has died.

She stared at her hands on the steering wheel. "I had no right to say the things I did. I'm sure your parents do what they think best."

I saw Miss then. A woman who loved my sister. Someone who loved me. I started to tell her not to worry. I hadn't listened to most of what she'd said anyway. For a moment, I thought she might even hug me. But in that second she exploded again. "It's just stupid to send a child into a foreign country on a bus!"

If lightning had hit the van, it would've been better. I wanted to say, *Mamá ISN'T stupid!* I wanted to say, *Mexico isn't a foreign country—it's HOME!*

Mostly I wanted to say, *What about ME?*

All those words fought to get out of my mouth at the same time. They stuck in my throat, and before any of them came, I jumped out of the van and ran down the stairwell to our apartment.

I thought I'd feel better when Rosa got home. But when she came in with Papi, new little silver stars glinted from her ears. She'd spent Christmas with Mamá, and I hadn't.

I wasn't going to speak to Rosa, but she pulled me into our room and closed the door. From her underwear drawer, she pulled out a wrapped package. *The sweater.* "I forgot to give this to you before I left to go to the—to Mexico. It is from Miss and me."

I shoved it back at her.

She didn't seem angry, or even surprised. She

put the package on my bed, then turned to me. "Miss was right."

I snorted. *Isn't she always?*

"We are not Mexicans."

Her words were plain, but I couldn't wrap my mind around them. I shook my head like a dog with water in its ear.

"When I was in Mexico, it was as though I had never seen it. It is dirty. A cat died, and was left in the street to rot and stink."

Can this be true?

"I washed my hair in the sink, and one of our uncles yelled about 'wasting water.' The people have nothing. We would not know how to live there."

I forgot I wasn't speaking to her. "You're lying."

"At the funeral, people pointed and whispered, saying I was Abuelita's rich American granddaughter."

"We're not rich!"

"Our uncles think we are. They want money to pay Abuelita's doctor bills. Mamá told them we do not have it, but they saw my braces."

I sank onto the edge of my bed. "Your braces were free!"

"Mamá told them, but they do not believe her. They say she is American now and does not care about family. They have to sell the farm to get the money."

Again I opened my mouth to speak, but my tongue was dry. In a moment—in less than a moment—the happy picture of our family living together on Abuelita's farm vanished. The future was dark, scary, filled with only questions. If Mexico wasn't home, I was lost.

Like in that movie. Dorothy after the twister. Lost with no ruby slippers.

I swallowed. "We're Americans?"

Rosa sat on her bed, looking at the carpet. "No. We are not Americans."

"W-where do we belong?"

She looked into my eyes. Into my soul. "Here. In the barrio of northeast Maplewood."

Miss was right again. Our world was too small.

* * *

The only good thing about Abuelita's death was that Mamá could come home. I hung on to that the way a little kid in the deep end of the pool hangs on to his floaties. So he doesn't drown.

Papi sent money to Mamá.

Then we waited.

"WHY CAN'T I do my driving with Dad? His car's smaller," Ethan whined.

Miss sighed. "You ask such easy questions. Your dad's not going to let you drive his precious car. Ask me something hard — like, *Hey, Mom, why don't you drop me off at the nearest bus stop?*"

Ethan snorted. French was a private language between Miss and me, but Ethan and his mom spoke in *sarcasm*. Behind the steering wheel, his head swiveled, scanning the street in front of our apartment. The turn signal continued its *click-click-click*, counting off the seconds. In the seat next to him, Miss sat with her "patient" look.

He eased the van into the street. "This thing's a boat. It's like trying to pilot the USS *Enterprise*."

At sixteen, Ethan looked too small to be driving, especially something as large as the van. But that's not why I was amazed.

Ethan was afraid to drive. And he didn't care that we knew. Boys in our neighborhood could be scared sometimes, but only little ones would admit it.

Rosa grinned. "Ethan, you are such a weenie!"

Miss shot her a look, and Rosa's grin disappeared.

I was glad Miss made Rosa "put a sock in it," as Ethan would say. No other boy I knew was brave enough to be afraid.

But if driving a car was the scariest thing Ethan had to do, he was lucky. Even after months with Miss, I still had fears, but not about stupid stuff like taking French or girls in gymnastics class. Real fears.

Mamá had tried to cross *la línea* once already. She was looking for another guide to help her, because the first one got shot in the knee. When they took Mamá back to Mexico, *la migra*—the border police—brought the injured man to a hospital.

His joint was shattered. He'd live, but he might not walk again.

No one said it. Not Papi, or Rosa, or Tía, or me. But we all thought it. *That could've been Mamá who was shot.*

I was afraid to go to bed. The last several mornings, Papi found Rosa and me asleep on the sofa with the television on. Each time we lied and told him we got caught up in a movie. He bawled us out, telling us we needed our sleep for school. I couldn't tell him the truth—that I'd been having nightmares about men in uniforms with guns.

Rosa and I wouldn't talk about our dreams. Not even to each other. That would make them too real. We walked around with fear in our bellies and worry in our minds.

Miss leaned forward from the passenger seat and tapped the middle of the windshield with her left hand.

Ethan flicked on the turn signal and took the next left.

She leaned forward and tapped the right side of the windshield. Ethan turned right.

It went on like that. No one said anything until we got to the recreation center. Miss took the keys and walked inside. Rosa and Ethan followed.

I blocked Cody's path. "Why did your mom do that? Tap on the window? Why wouldn't she talk to him?"

"Ethan has ADD—Attention Deficit Disorder." Cody said it like that explained everything. But he must've read the confusion in my face. "He has trouble focusing, remembering right, left, east, west. So Mom taps on the glass."

"Ethan told me he's a genius. He's—*disabled*?"

"He's both."

I didn't know what to think about that. Ethan seemed so smart sometimes. Like when he was making movies or inventing new games. But it was true that other times his big ideas got us into trouble. Those were the times when Miss said he was *impulsive*. But I still didn't understand what that meant.

Cody read my face. He shrugged. "Ethan is Ethan."

*   *   *

Inside the rec center, Rosa went swimming with Ethan and Cody. Miss watched as I did gymnastics.

It'd begun as something fun to do, but gymnastics had become something more. It took my mind off my fears when days passed with no word from Mamá. You can't do a forward roll on the balance beam and be thinking of something else. A human brain isn't big enough.

It seemed wrong to force Mamá from my mind. But thinking about her made me curl into a ball of pain. Papi found me once, hiding under his bedcovers. He gathered me into his arms, like I was still little. For that moment, I was completely safe. I wanted him to hold me like that forever.

He told me not to worry. "Your *mamá*'s smart. She's crossed *la línea* many times, *sí*? We need to be patient — to be strong like your *mamá*."

But afterward he stayed in his room with the door closed for a long time. His eyes were red when he came out.

I wanted to be strong. For him. I tried to wait.

But I found myself checking my watch, counting days on the calendar, acting just like Miss. I realized why she hated waiting. The terrible thing about waiting is *there's no way to do it faster.*

Miss's *influence* took over other parts of my life, too. The fun and freedom of flipping around in gymnastics gave way to a different feeling—the power of making my body *perform.*

My hunger for control spilled into the rest of my life. I did *not* want to be someone things just happened to. I wanted to be the one to make them happen.

Someone like my mentor.

Life was about to remind me that *feeling* in control and actually *having* control are two different things.

When Rosa and I walked into our apartment after getting home from the recreation center, everything seemed normal.

But Suelita should've been sitting in the living room with animal crackers and a juice box. There should've been cartoons on the TV. The smell of rice and beans should've been hanging in the air.

We should've heard the soft rumbling of Papi's sleep as he rested between his day and night jobs.

Our apartment had forgotten us. It'd been home when we'd left, a couple of hours before, but the rooms were suddenly strangers. We walked through the silence to find Papi's bed empty.

Rosa swallowed her panic. I watched the lump slide right down her throat. Then she said, "Papi's probably still at Tía's."

So I gulped down my panic, too. The fear hitting my stomach almost made me sick. But it was easier than facing the truth.

For almost one whole day we pretended that everything was fine. Rosa called Tía to see if Papi was there. *Maybe he has to fix something? Isn't Tía's faucet leaking?*

When Tía said he hadn't come for Suelita, we pretended he had to pick up a few things at the store. When we tried to call and he didn't answer, we told each other his phone needed charging.

Rosa and I walked to Tia's to get Suelita. After we made dinner, we left Papi's meal on a plate with another plate over it so he could eat it when he got home.

We pretended to do our homework, glancing out of the corners of our eyes at the phone. Our ears strained to hear his footsteps coming down the stairwell. We went to bed and pretended to sleep.

The next morning his cold plate of food was still on the table. Neither of us moved it. That would be bad luck.

Rosa scrambled some eggs for breakfast, but that was the only thing that was normal. She brewed coffee as a special treat, but we couldn't drink it. It stayed bitter even with the milk and sugar she stirred into it. We each took a sip and pushed it away.

Same kitchen, same breakfast. But without Mamá and Papi, it wasn't home.

Papi would've taken Suelita to Tía's, then gone to his day job. We should've done that—taken Suelita to Tía Carmen's and gone to school. But we decided to stay home, watch Suelita, and wait for Papi. We gave ourselves the excuse that we hadn't slept well. *Maybe we're coming down with colds?*

It was good that we were tired. Otherwise anyone who came down the stairwell could've looked through our front window and seen us watching TV. If we'd been talking, they would've heard us through the apartment walls.

But my sisters and I were cuddled together on Mamá and Papi's bed, asleep.

BAM! BAM! BAM! "POLICE! ANYBODY HOME?"

I sat up, too scared to cry out.

BAM! BAM! BAM!

Suelita filled her lungs to emit a shriek.

Rosa clamped her hand over our sister's mouth. Suelita clawed Rosa's arm with her sharp little nails, but Rosa hung on.

Like our lives depended on it.

The pounding on the door stopped, but my heart kept hammering. The three of us froze.

"HELLO? ANYONE THERE?"

Rosa and I stared at each other, eyes wild, not breathing.

"MAPLEWOOD POLICE, LOOKING FOR THE JUÁREZ RESIDENCE?"

Suelita thrashed.

"*¡Silencio!*" Rosa hissed.

I grabbed Suelita's hands to stop her from tearing Rosa's skin.

The pounding on the door continued.

I winced at each blow. *Will he kick the door open? Like on television?*

Silence.

Slowly Rosa removed her hand from our sister's red face. Suelita drew a long, gasping breath. She whimpered but stifled the sound and turned away when Rosa moved to cover her mouth again.

Heavy footfalls reverberated up the stairwell, the sound dying away.

We waited. I felt dizzy until I remembered to breathe.

What's happened to Papi? Will they take us to foster care?

I whispered, "What do they want?"

"*Shh!*" Rosa hissed, listening to the stillness.

BAM! BAM! BAM!

The bed bounced as we jumped. A small squeal escaped my lips. We turned to see a shadow on the sheet covering the high basement window across the room from us.

"POLICE! ANYONE HOME? LOOKING FOR THE JUÁREZ FAMILY!"

Rosa and I stared in terror. Suelita clapped her hands over her eyes. Except for our racing hearts, we were paralyzed. Statues.

My blood whooshed in my ears. Like a washing machine.

The shadow on the curtain hesitated. Then moved away.

Minutes passed. We didn't speak, didn't move. Finally our muscles loosened and we lay back against the softness of our parents' bed. Suelita rolled to her side, into Rosa's warmth, burrowing there, whimpering.

Tears dripped down my face.

Rosa reached out and rubbed my shoulder. I saw the scratches from Suelita's nails on her arm.

"We need to call Miss," I said.

Rosa shook her head. "We need to go to Tía's."

BUT THE NEXT DAY I did call Miss. Papi told me to. And that shows how desperate he was.

He'd been arrested for a burned-out taillight. He'd tried calling our apartment from the jail and was worried when we didn't answer. He sounded relieved to find us at Tía's.

I was so relieved, just hearing his voice, that my eyes started leaking. When I'd finally fallen asleep the night before, lying head to toe with Rosa on Tía's sofa, I dreamed of the porch at Angélica's old apartment. The place where her *papá* died.

It was splattered in red.

We told Papi we'd gone to Tia's because the police had come to our door. He worried and wondered how they'd known where to find us. He was careful not to carry anything with our address on it.

We huddled together—my aunt, my sisters, and me—straining to hear him through Tía's ancient speakerphone. Waiting for him to tell us what to do.

"Call Miss," he'd said.

Rosa and I exchanged looks. *Did I hear right?* Papi had warned me many times not to tell Miss anything. *Now he wants me to call her?* But when I thought about it, it made sense. The thing we'd been afraid of had already happened. And if anyone could fix it, that person was Miss.

Tears streamed down our faces as Papi said he loved us. I wanted to say so many things, but my words stuck like a chicken bone, tearing the inside of my throat.

When Tía said good-bye to Papi, her voice broke with fear. I'd always thought of her as a grown-up, but just then I realized that she was younger than Papi—a lot younger—and that being left alone with the six of us kids was too much for anyone.

She pushed the phone at me as she echoed Papi's words. "Call Miss."

My hands shook when I took the handset from her. I wanted to take it to another room, but the phone was the old-fashioned kind, with a cord attached to the base. So I took it off speakerphone and called Miss's cell. I turned away from Rosa, worried that she might still overhear.

From far away I heard the tinny version of Miss's musical voice. "Carmen?"

"No, Miss, it's me. I—we need your help. Papi's in jail."

A pause.

"What! Why?"

"He—his car had a burned-out taillight."

Miss snorted. "They don't—"

Nothing.

"Miss? Are you there?"

Her voice choked. "You—you *lied*? To *me*? Why?"

Rosa clapped her hands to her forehead. Even without the speakerphone on, she heard every word.

My face burned. I let Miss's question hang in the air until the answer became obvious.

"You didn't trust me." Her voice was full of

hurt. The pain traveled through the phone line, into my ears.

I knew I should feel guilty, but right then I was mad. This wasn't about Miss. It was about *my* family. "We need to save Papi! Are you going to help us, or not?"

I listened to Miss breathe. "I need to think about this."

I heard the click as she hung up.

Rosa shouted, "You lied? Miss will never help us now! All because of you!"

I was afraid Rosa was right. Miss hated being lied to. I worried that she wouldn't come.

But she did. In minutes she stood at Tía's door.

"What about your work?" I asked.

"Maury will have to get over it." But her face was worried.

Then she paced around Tía's living room all morning, making phone calls, trying to get answers to what was happening to Papi. But we still had only questions.

Miss dropped her phone into her bag and sighed. "We're going to have to drive down to the holding facility. One of you needs to go with me. I want to talk to your dad, and I might need a translator."

Both Rosa and I wanted to help rescue Papi. I saw the hurt in Rosa's eyes when Miss said my English skills were a bit better.

I wore the Christmas sweater they bought me. Even though it was pink, I didn't want to wear it. Not until Mamá came home. But I had no choice. When I'd slipped into Mamá's old sweater, Miss said, "I'm not taking you to a federal office wearing that grungy thing. Those people need to know your dad's a good parent."

She told Tía and Rosa to keep trying to reach Mamá, even though we'd explained we had to wait until Mamá called us.

Then we rumbled away in a cloud of blue smoke. After we left Tía's, Miss insisted that we stop by our apartment to get my passport. I didn't want to take the time to look for the stupid thing. I'd only used the little blue booklet once, on my visit to Mexico. We finally found it in the cookie jar on top of the refrigerator.

Once we were on our way again, I used the

button to open the van window. The icy blast made it feel like we were racing. Rushing to rescue Papi. For once I was glad Miss had a *lead foot*.

"Roll that window up. You'll mess my hair."

Nothing but a hurricane could've made her hair move, but I rolled up the window.

She was wearing her TV clothes. A skinny brown skirt and a copper jacket that matched her hair. She looked ready to burst into flame, rich and important.

When I told her, she said, "Good. Maybe they'll think I'm a lawyer."

"It won't work. They'll recognize you."

"Even better. These ICE officials are a scary bunch."

"Ice?"

"Immigration and Customs Enforcement."

Ice was the right name for people who'd take Papi away.

The snow had mostly melted, sucked back into the dry Colorado air, but piles of dirty slush lined the streets. The sun beat down on the dead grass and naked trees.

Except for Christmas and snow days, I never

liked winter. It was messy, muddy, full of ugly shades of brown.

But the golden sunshine, water-blue skies, and Miss in her fiery colors filled me with hope. She would fix this.

We rolled up to a flat building with a metal roof. It didn't look like a jail. More like a warehouse. A warehouse filled with people waiting to be shipped out.

I tiptoed past the heavy metal door. Like the cowardly lion who asked the wizard for courage in that movie.

The door clanged shut behind us. The fluorescent light made everything look cold. Like ice. My knees started knocking into each other, something I'd thought only happened in cartoons. *Maybe I should've let Rosa come instead.*

The guard stood over me—a man with a gun on his hip and a badge on his uniform. Standing in the cold light of a room with no air in it, his creamy light brown skin looked blue-white. I clutched my pink purse to my chest, now glad to have my passport inside it. I didn't feel like an American, but the blue book was proof.

"We're looking for Miguel Juárez," Miss said to the guard.

"You know his number?"

She frowned. "No."

"We might have several detainees named Miguel Juárez."

Miss sighed. "I called this morning and was told I had to come here to get his number."

"Are you a relative?"

Her throat turned red, but it looked purple in the blue light. "This is his daughter."

He did something *unexpected*. He smiled at me. A warm, reassuring smile. I didn't think an ICE man could smile like that. Suddenly he looked like Mr. Flores, my Language Arts teacher. Then the smile melted like the snow. "We could try looking up his birth date."

Miss looked at me, and I told them Papi's birthday. But when the man asked, I didn't know what year he was born.

"How old is he?" the guard asked.

"Thirty-three."

The guard typed numbers into his computer while I listened to the hum of the flickering lights. I tried to look through the window of another metal door but couldn't see past the glare and the chicken wire in the glass.

How can someone so close be so far away?

It turned out that he wasn't even back there, but at the time I was ready to break down the door with my fists. Instead I slipped a hand into Miss's, wrapping my pinkie around her pointer finger. She gave me a grimace that was *not* reassuring. The guard stopped typing and stared at the screen.

"Nothing. Sorry." He looked at me, and I saw his soul.

He is sorry. ICE men must have daughters, too.

"He's not here?" asked Miss.

"Well, if he is, he's not in the computer."

"It's been two days!"

The guard shrugged. "I don't know what to tell you."

"Surely there's some kind of record."

"You might check the field office."

Another long drive. Another government building, but newer and taller. We walked through a glass door. It looked like Miss's bank, with shiny stone walls, and a ceiling far away. People waited on chairs in rows. It didn't look as scary as the warehouse.

That shows not to trust *first impressions.*

Two officers worked behind a desk. They both had guns and badges. The hairs on the back of my neck stood up.

The large woman in uniform said, "May I help you."

It didn't sound like a question. She was talking to us, but it was hard to tell. Her eyes were rolled up toward the ceiling, though she must have seen it before. I wondered if she had a string in the back of her neck you pulled to make her talk like that.

"We're looking for a detainee," said Miss.

"Fill out a request form." The woman shoved a paper at us, still staring at the ceiling.

I thought of what Miss had said about looking people in the eye. And I understood. The guard was being *disrespectful.* Telling us we didn't exist.

Miss slapped her purse on the desk. She pulled out a pen and snapped the bag shut again. She was annoyed, but the guard didn't seem to know or care how dangerous Miss could be.

She'll find out.

I looked at the people sitting in rows. Not just Mexicans. People in all different colors. Women with children, tired old men, angry young men. People by themselves, and whole families talking in languages I didn't know.

Are all of them waiting to see their fathers, brothers, sons? Are there women detainees, too?

Miss's voice broke into my thoughts. "I don't have his number. That's why we're here."

The guard dragged her eyes from the ceiling and looked Miss up and down. "Are you a family member?"

The guard was big, taller than my mentor, but Miss lifted her chin. "This is the man's *daughter.*"

The way she said it made me sound important. As though being the daughter of Miguel Juárez was like being a queen. So I lifted *my* chin.

The guard gave me what's called a *withering*

look. I dropped my eyes to the floor. *You can just keep your nasty eyes on the ceiling!*

"If you're his daughter, you should have his number," she said.

I recognized her tone. It's called *derisive.*

Miss stepped between me and the guard, showing all her teeth. It wasn't a smile. She reminded me of a mother bear on a nature channel. "As I said, we're here to *get* his number."

"I'm sorry." The guard looked back at the ceiling.

It felt like a slap in the face, and I realized the conversation was *over.*

"I need to talk with a supervisor," said Miss.

"Do you have an appointment?" the guard asked the ceiling.

"No. I need to talk to your supervisor."

The guard flicked her eyes at Miss. "I said, you need an appointment."

"I heard you. I want to make a complaint."

We followed the woman down a hall. She mumbled, "If I get into trouble over this—"

But Miss enjoyed making trouble for rude people.

The big woman made Miss take off her watch, her earrings, and her shoes when we went through a metal detector. I could tell the guard enjoyed that. She took the nail file she found in Miss's purse and threw it in a trash can. She glanced into my purse and handed it back to me. Then we were marched down a passageway.

Another man stepped out of an office. His name tag said ARELLANO. "May I help you?"

Miss held out her hand. "Kathryn Dawson Dahl."

His eyes widened.

"May we sit down?" Miss asked.

Mr. Arellano smiled the way Miss did some-times—the smile-that-wasn't-a-smile—and he didn't take her hand. "I'm afraid not, Mrs. Dahl. I do not have clearance to talk to the media."

The lady guard's eyes moved from the ceiling to Miss. As though she'd just noticed her.

I grinned.

"I'm not here with 5News," Miss told him.

"It wouldn't be worth my job to risk it. Surely you understand."

Miss blew a whiff of air out her nose. "The

station has no idea I'm here. I told them I'm out with a sick child."

I turned to stare at Miss. *She lied to the people at her work? Miss says lying is for cowards.* But maybe it wasn't a lie. I *was* sick—sick with worry.

Mr. Arellano gave a little nod. "What's on your mind?"

"We're looking for a detainee. Your people are unable to locate him in your system."

"You are family?"

"This is his daughter."

"You have his case number?" Mr. Arellano looked at me, but I looked at the floor.

Miss answered for me. "We've been trying to get his number all morning."

I looked up at him. I wanted to use my puppy-dog eyes, but I couldn't do it. Now that I knew about real power, it felt like cheating.

Mr. Arellano showed all his white teeth. He turned his smile on me. "If your father's been detained, he would've been allowed to make a phone call. If he hasn't called you, there's nothing I can do."

His fake smile made me mad. Miss had warned me to let her do the talking, but I blurted, "He did call! But he didn't give us a case number, and no one told him where he is!"

Mr. Arellano spread his hands apart and shrugged. "I'm sorry."

I didn't have to see his soul to know that he wasn't.

Miss didn't try to hide her annoyance. "Walk me through your procedure."

"It depends on the circumstances."

"Such as?"

"Mrs. Dahl, I don't have time to talk you through multiple scenarios."

"A typical scenario. Is there a hearing? Are they posted somewhere?"

"I'm sorry. You need to leave."

I stiffened.

"I'm invoking the Freedom of Information Act." Her voice had a sharp edge. Like broken glass.

"You need to leave," he repeated.

"What do I do? Write a letter? To whom?"

Mr. Arellano folded his arms across his chest.

Miss crossed her own arms. "I asked you a question."

His eyes flashed, but his voice was *calm*. Like a dead man's voice. "You think I haven't seen your kind before? Well-meaning church ladies. You take a barrio kid out for ice cream once a week and think you're Mother Teresa."

My mouth hung open. *What Mexican would talk to a white lady like that?* But then it hit me. Mr. Arellano wasn't Mexican. He was American.

And he wasn't through with Miss. "You charge in here, demanding special treatment for your charity of the week. You think I don't know what these kids go through? I see it every day. If you don't like it, then change the law. But don't barge in here and tell me how to do my job."

I glanced at Miss. Her eyes were wide and round. I was sure nobody had ever spoken to her that way before.

"Mrs. Dahl, you have been asked *twice* to leave a high-security area. Walk out now, or be arrested."

The big guard took a step. The handcuffs on her belt clinked. I grabbed Miss's hand. It trembled in mine. I thought I was shivering, until I realized, *Miss is the one shaking!* I looked at her face and saw something I'd never seen there before.

Fear.

She tried to say something, but the strangled sound wasn't English. Mr. Arellano made a motion to the guard, but before the big woman could move, we were halfway down the hall.

Miss dragged me along. Her usually cool hand was sweaty. The guard harangued us — like a pit bull barking and snapping at our heels. I didn't hear what she said. My heart throbbed like a drum in my ears.

After we burst through the doorway to the outside, words burst out of me. "Miss, could they really arrest you?"

"Get in the van."

Once inside, she leaned against the steering wheel with her eyes closed, taking deep breaths.

"Miss, they *couldn't* really arrest you!"

She looked at me, shaking her head. "Put it on my tombstone."

"You just asked a question!" I wanted her to

think *logically,* to storm back in there and fight. It was a luxury only *she* could afford.

Then I realized I was wrong.

I'm an American. I can go back in there and stand up for myself. Like in the French class. I unbuckled my seat belt, but before I could open the door, Miss grabbed my arm.

"Jacinta, I'm tapped out. If we get arrested, I can't afford another lawyer."

"Call your TV people!"

"So I can get *fired?* I told them I was out with a sick kid, remember?"

"SO YOU DO *NOTHING?*"

"Nothing?"

"Think of something!"

Her breathing had returned to normal, but her face was still red. "Thinking and adrenaline are a bad mix."

I'd learned in science that adrenaline triggers the fight-or-flight response. *I* wanted to fight, but Miss seemed ready to run away. I'd thought she was brave.

But if you're brave only when you know you're safe, are you ever really brave at all?

Then her eyebrows pulled together, and she stared out the windshield. I could tell she was trying. I shut up so she could think.

My heartbeat slowed until I couldn't feel it in my ears anymore. It was cold outside, but sun streamed through the glass like in the botanic garden's greenhouse. I was steaming. I took off my new sweater and looked at it.

I knew it was bad luck to leave Mamá's sweater behind!

I threw the new one on the van floor.

Miss didn't notice.

I looked to see what she was staring at. A single leaf clinging to a tree in front of us danced in the breeze. I watched it play, watched it twirl.

Miss can fix this. I couldn't let myself think anything else. *She'll call somebody. The mayor, or maybe the governor.*

We watched the leaf until the wind tore it away.

Miss must've heard my thoughts. "I could call

our senator. She could make Mr. Arellano's life pretty miserable. But that might make things worse."

"Worse?"

"For your dad."

A chill went through me. *Papi? What could they do him? Did we give Mr. Arellano his name? Would he find Papi and hurt him?* "WHAT ARE WE GOING TO DO?"

Her face was whiter than I'd ever seen it. I saw freckles under her makeup.

She whispered, "I don't know."

25

MISS STARTED the engine and backed away from the ICE building, but her eyes were empty.

How can she drive without seeing?

If her head had been made of glass, I would've seen wheels turning inside. I waited for a spark—a light to come into her eyes—but it didn't happen. The stone in my stomach got heavier.

I thought I might throw up.

I pushed the little button to open the window and stared at the slushy gray mounds on the roadside. Even with cold air blowing on me, sweat poured off my face.

Miss said nothing, even when I started shivering. I felt sick, like I had a fever. I thought about putting my new sweater back on, but I was afraid of the jinx.

Why isn't Miss ordering me to roll up the window?

Finally I closed it myself.

We were on the street to Tía's apartment when the van turned. I looked at Miss for an answer. She pulled into the youth center parking lot. In a few minutes I was in Mrs. E.'s office with a glass of soda in front of me. Diet.

"Sorry for not calling, Liz. We were driving by when I realized you might be able to help."

Mrs. Espinosa sat on the sofa next to me. "What's going on?"

Miss looked at me. "Jacinta?"

Does everyone have to know? It felt like the word was stamped across my forehead in big red letters. ILLEGAL.

Mrs. E.'s small dog—who usually slept in the corner of her office—got up on stiff little legs and trotted over to sniff my hands, which were suddenly wet. I wiped them on my jeans. I wanted Mamá, Papi. Someone to tell me what to do. I picked up the soda and took a sip so my mouth wouldn't be dry, but my eyes started leaking.

"Was your dad deported?" Mrs. E. whispered.

As though asking softly would make it hurt less.

I nodded, holding the glass to my lips so I wouldn't have to talk.

Miss said, "Well, not yet, anyway. Miguel called his sister this morning. He's been detained, but he didn't leave a case number, and he doesn't know where he's being held. We went to the ICE regional office and got stonewalled."

Mrs. Espinosa frowned. "You went down there?"

Miss pressed her lips together and nodded.

Mrs. E. sighed. "You need to be careful, Kate. Sometimes those folks play rough. It could come back on Miguel."

Miss flinched. "That's what I'm afraid of. What happens now?"

"There should be a hearing," said Mrs. E.

"Does he get a lawyer? What happens to the girls?"

Mrs. Espinosa stood up. "How would you ladies like some cookies?"

Why do grown-ups ask the stupidest questions at the worst times? I was left sitting *outside* Mrs. E.'s office with a plate of stale animal crackers and my watery diet soda. All the ice had melted.

I could see them through the office windows. Both ladies had cups of coffee, and their heads were together. *My papi* had been taken away, but *I* was dumped in the waiting room with the dog.

To Americans, I'm just some Mexican. My whole family—a bunch of dumb Mexicans. Go ahead and shoot us like dogs.

Mrs. E.'s little dog whined through his lips. I picked him up and held him. His tiny tongue tried to kiss away my tears.

Don't worry, I thought to him. *Americans don't really shoot dogs.*

After a million years the ladies walked out of Mrs. E.'s office.

"Come on, Jacinta, we need to get to your aunt's," said Miss.

I was slow getting up. I didn't thank Mrs. Espinosa, and I didn't say good-bye. They were whispering to each other as we walked outside, so they didn't notice. Or didn't care.

"Tread lightly," Mrs. Espinosa said in Miss's ear.

Miss nodded, and we got in the car. As soon as Mrs. E. turned to walk back inside, I yanked the keys from the ignition.

"Jacin—" Miss's voice broke off when she looked at my face.

"What did Mrs. Espinosa say?"

Miss stared at her lap. "She doesn't know what will happen to you girls. Sometimes kids are deported with their parents. Sometimes they go into foster care."

A bomb went off in my brain.

But Miss didn't hear the explosion inside my head, so she kept talking. "Sometimes when parents are deported, their kids just—disappear." She swallowed. "Your aunt's not able to take care of all three of you. I—I'm thinking that you and Rosa should live with me for a while."

"We need to get Papi back!"

Miss whispered, "I don't know if we can."

I threw myself against the car seat, pounding my fist on the window, making the van rock.

Miss jumped. "Jacinta!"

"How can a person's life be fine one minute and destroyed the next?" I didn't realize I'd asked the question out loud until I heard Miss answer.

"I don't know. Maybe Gerald Benton turned your dad in. To get back at me for embarrassing him in front of the city manager."

It was a punch in the stomach. *I have no parents because of gymnastics?*

Papi said he'd been stopped for a taillight. *But the next day a policeman came to our apartment!* I struggled to breathe. "You think Mr. Benton called the police?"

"Not really. I'm grabbing at straws. But somehow the police knew where to find you girls. And that worries me." She took the keys from me and started the engine.

"WHAT ARE WE GOING TO *DO*?"

Miss looked at me. I saw her lips moving, but the sounds weren't hers. They were the tones of a lost little girl. A voice like my own.

"I don't know."

The second time she'd said that to me. The second time in the same day.

WHEN WE GOT to Tía's apartment, Rosa was watching from the window. She ran to the van before Miss switched off the engine. "Papi called again. He gave us his case number."

Miss frowned. "Why didn't you call me?"

"I did. You did not answer."

Miss fumbled in her purse, then pulled out her phone. Looking at it, she groaned, then dropped it back in her purse. "All right, let's get inside."

My cousins ran into their bedroom to hide when Miss walked in. Suelita buried her face in the sofa. Tía's and Rosa's eyes were red.

Someone has to be strong. Someone has to get Papi back.

"Miguel is in the Teller County Jail," Tía told us.

Miss asked, "Teller County? Why Teller?"

"We need to go get him," I said.

Miss turned to me. "Do you have any idea where Teller County is?"

"No," Rosa and I answered together.

"Drive south for two hours and hang a right. It's halfway into the mountains." Miss asked Rosa, "Have you heard from your mother?"

"I talked to her brothers, but they do not know where she is. They have not heard from her since she left for America."

I filled up with fear. I wanted to tear off my skin so I wouldn't have to feel anymore.

Miss took a deep breath, then let it out. "I need to know what your parents want for you girls."

She pulled out her phone and started pushing buttons.

Finally! Someone is doing something. I took deep breaths, trying to quiet my heart. So I could listen.

"Colorado. Teller County Jail," Miss said into the phone. She wasn't a little girl anymore.

Yes, Miss, DO something. You have to, you HAVE to!

After a short conversation she dropped her phone back into her purse again. "He's in Teller because of the overflow in Denver. They won't let me talk to him on the phone. I need to go down there."

"I'm coming with you," I said.

"No. After talking with Liz Espinosa, I'm worried what could happen if they know where to find you girls."

I shouted, "I don't care! I'm not letting you mess up again."

"*Mess up?* I'm trying to *help*. If your dad's deported, you might get stuck in foster care." She drew a breath. "Maybe it's best if you live with me for a while."

"If Papi's deported, I'm going with him! I'm not staying with *YOU*!" All the times I'd daydreamed of being Miss's daughter flashed through my guilty mind.

Fear flickered in her eyes. I knew she didn't want

Rosa and me going to Mexico. She still thought she knew what was best for us.

Her throat was red, but her voice was calm. "That's your dad's decision." She turned to go.

My world tilted like a nightmare. I staggered after her. "Wait!"

She walked out the door and down the steps.

I chased her. Tried to make my words quiet, powerful. "Let's think about this—"

But she opened the van door.

"IF YOU LEAVE WITHOUT ME, I'LL *HATE* YOU. I'LL NEVER SEE YOU AGAIN!"

She got in, slammed the door, and the locks clicked.

I made it to the passenger side and pounded on the window before Tía and Rosa caught me. I threw off my aunt's hand and bloodied Rosa's nose, but they dragged me back onto the curb.

A dog barked. Through my tangle of hair I saw someone across the street pull back a curtain to stare. Suelita and my cousins spilled out of Tía's apartment, adding their shrieks to mine.

"Stop! *Please, stop!*" My words were strangled by sobs.

The van pulled away.

"I hate you! I HATE YOU!"

I screamed long after Tía and Rosa released me. Long after the van was gone.

27

MISS FUSSED in front of the mirror in Tía's tiny bathroom while I read the notes Miss had written for her testimony at Papi's hearing. The note card on the top of the stack said:

> Miguel Juárez is a hardworking man, the sole support of three minor daughters who are U.S. citizens. Sending him to Mexico would impose a hardship not only on the Juárez family but also on the Maplewood community and society as a whole.

I threw the stack of notes down on the table, scattering them. "This is stupid! Take me with you!"

"I already told you—your dad said no. Child Protective Services doesn't know anything about you girls. He wants to keep it that way." Rosa had gathered up the note cards I'd thrown. I grabbed them from her.

"No!" She tried to snatch them back.

I crumpled them. Ripped them.

Tía stood with her hand to her mouth. My cousins squealed. Miss came out of the bathroom and stood with her hands on her hips. "Luckily I've memorized what I'm going to say."

For hours Rosa and I slunk from room to room in Tía's apartment, like snipers in a video game. Our fears *ricocheted* off the walls, hitting Suelita and our cousins like bullets. They cried and fought with each other until they collapsed.

Tía rocked on the sofa, hugging the baby to her, staring with empty eyes.

I imagined Papi standing before the judge, so brave. Papi never showed fear. But he'd often been worried. Then I realized that worry *is* fear — the fear of things that haven't happened yet.

We still hadn't heard from Mamá. I threw myself across Tía's big bed, squeezing my eyes shut, my sweaty hands gripping each other. *Please, God, please.* I didn't put my thoughts into words, couldn't let myself think about what might be happening to Mamá. Forming the words might make them come true.

When her van pulled up, we didn't run to Miss. Rosa and I stared through the window, searching for some sign, a reason to hope. Clutching the baby to her chest, Carmen struggled to her feet.

Miss dragged herself out of the van, her face down.

Tía's legs buckled. She fell back onto the sofa, sobbing.

Of course the judge didn't care what Miss had to say! She's nobody! I could've convinced the judge to let Papi go, but I never had the chance, and it's HER fault! She put our address on the recreation form. She made Mr. Benton and Mr. Arellano angry. Miss used her power for stupid things, like swimming and gymnastics, and let Papi be deported!

I was ready to say these things to Miss. If I didn't say them, my mouth would burst into flames.

But as Miss reached the screen door to Tía's

apartment, Rosa turned on me. "This is *your* fault! *YOU* had to take gymnastics!"

My fire sputtered as if Rosa had thrown a bucket of water.

Miss came in without knocking. "Girls, please. This is nobody's fault."

"It's your fault!" I hurled at Miss.

"No, *YOU*!" Rosa threw back at me. "You *LIED* to Miss about Papi having papers! Just so YOU could take gymnastics. Everything has to be about YOU!"

My brain shut down.

By itself, my arm came around in a wide circle. All my anger, all my pain, all my *guilt* was in that arm.

The rest of me was empty.

I didn't wait to see Rosa slump to the carpet. I bolted for the bathroom, threw myself against the door, then locked it. Miss and Tía shouted in different languages, yelling at each other to get ice for my sister's face.

My strength seeped out of me, and I slid to the floor. The door reverberated as Miss pounded on it. "Jacinta, get out here!"

"You're not my *mamá*! *You're not*! YOU'RE NOT!" Sobbing, I stepped into the tub. That was as far from Miss as I could get. I cried so hard, I started hiccuping. My head pounded, and I couldn't catch my breath. I wiped my face with my hands. Staring through the grimy, wavy glass of the bathroom window, I tried to make sense of the warped skeletons of trees outside.

Dead insects dotted the window ledge.

A tiny movement drew my eyes to a fat spider in the corner of the sill. She gloated over the dried bodies of a family of pill bugs.

Miss called through the door, her voice raspy, "Jacinta! We can't stop the bleeding. I'm taking Rosa to the emergency room."

The hospital? Victor's scarred face flashed in my mind. *No! I'm not like him! That's not who I am!*

The front door slammed. A minute later came the wheezy sound of the van pulling away.

I squashed the spider with my thumb. "This is her fault."

*   *   *

When Miss returned with Rosa, I retreated again into the bathroom. Through the door, I listened as Miss spoke to Tía about having my sisters and me live with her until either Mamá or Papi came home. But Miss wasn't going to force Suelita to go.

"I'm not sure I can handle her, Carmen. She still screams at the sight of me."

Even through the door I heard the panic in my aunt's voice when she said it was up to us where we wanted to live.

But I knew there was really only one choice. With Victor gone, Tía had to work. Rosa had been the one to cut school and watch my cousins a few days a week so Tía could clean houses. Tía couldn't make it alone with so many small children and no one to help her. And we all knew it. *Rosa knew it!*

But when Miss left, Rosa was with her.

Hate welled up in me. Maybe I should've been more understanding. With Mamá gone, Rosa had to be *responsible* for more than a year. Maybe she needed a chance to be a kid for a while.

But that's not how I saw it.

Rosa's a traitor and a brat! She wants to live with Miss, riding the school bus with Ethan every day, like some lazy, rich white girl? She's going to play with Cody in the pool while I take care of four babies by myself?

I was a Juárez. I'd cling to Tía, Suelita, and my cousins. What else could I do? But our family was falling apart, and it was Miss's fault. It had to be.

It *had* to.

Because if it wasn't Miss's fault — then maybe — maybe it was mine.

28

LATHER BUBBLED OUT and dripped from the rim of the dishwasher. Water squeezed out of the corners of my eyes. But I wasn't going to call anyone for help. Especially not my *erstwhile* mentor. *I can figure this out myself.*

I popped the door open, and the sound of swishing water stopped. I crossed my fingers and took a peek, praying *not* to see the entire machine filled with foam. Again.

Sighing, I used the bowl to scoop out more bubbles, then dumped the lather into the sink, my bare feet slipping on the soapy floor. I'd started the dishwasher at the Dahls' house many times, but Tía didn't have any of the special powder stuff. So I'd used regular dishwashing liquid. I didn't know if it would work, so I added extra.

Miss had told me, "There are two ways to learn. The easy way and the hard way." The easy way is learning from *other* people's mistakes. I'd just learned a new lesson. The hard way.

The phone rang.

Why can't Miss leave me alone?

Taking the soapy bowl with me, I went to check the caller ID. Just in case.

I didn't recognize the number, but it was long distance, so I snatched it up, praying it was Mamá. "*¿Bueno?*"

"Jacinta? Why are you at your aunt's apartment? I've been calling and calling."

"*Angélica?* Where are you?"

"In California. Living with my uncle."

What? Why?

"Sorry I didn't say good-bye," she mumbled.

I realized I wasn't the only one guilty of pulling away. I squirmed. "'S okay."

"Why haven't you been home? Did you get evicted?" she asked.

A knife twisted in my heart. "Papi got deported."

"Oh."

Taking the phone with me, I returned to the dishwasher and scooped out another bowl of foam.

Pause.

I searched my mind for something normal to say. "So—how's California? Do you like your new school?"

I dumped the bubbles in the sink, so I wasn't sure if the gurgling noise came from the phone. "Angélica?"

Another sob. "Mamá and Tío are working—so I—I don't go to school anymore. I'm taking care of my brothers and cousins."

I heard them fighting in the background. After another pause, she added, "School's stupid, anyway. What good does it do?"

While Angélica talked, I set the bowl on the counter and edged into the living room. Suelita and my cousins were piled on the sofa like a litter of sleepy puppies, their eyes barely open. Voices drifted from the television. I tried to listen as Angélica spoke about being bored, being lonely, but other thoughts pushed into my brain while her words mixed with the sounds of the TV.

It was all just noise. Nothing made sense.

And then it did. Angélica's life—a life with no *papá* and no education—was about to become mine.

Shut up! SHUT UP! I don't want to hear it! I fought my panic. *I'm supposed to tell Angélica something. What am I supposed to tell her?*

"Angélica? Your mentor? I mean—your Amiga? She tried to call you. Why didn't you answer?"

"Mamá sold my phone. To buy our bus tickets."

"Oh."

"Can you tell Miss Linda I said hi?"

I didn't want to see Miss Linda again. I wanted to tell Angélica that rich white ladies become Amigas to make themselves feel good, not because they care about *us*. I wanted to tell her that they aren't really brave or strong. They just seem that way, because there's nothing in their world to be afraid of.

But instead I said, "Sure."

Pause.

"I should go," she said.

"Angélica? Your Amiga was better—better than mine." I needed to give her something. To let her win.

And it was the truth.

She took a big breath. "It doesn't matter, Jacinta."

I held the phone away from my face as the dial tone grated against my ear.

Miss and Rosa pulled up in the van. Almost every day they'd call or come by. *How can Rosa let Miss take Mamá's place?* I went into Tía's bathroom and locked the door. Again.

I listened as they carried in more stuff from our family's old apartment. Bags of toys and cans of food. Clothes for me and Suelita.

Miss's voice pierced the bathroom wall. "We found an eviction notice on the door."

Stunned, I sat down hard on the toilet. I realized I should've been expecting it.

Even though Tía's English was pretty good, Rosa translated Miss's words. "This is all we could fit in the van. Take Jacinta over there. Grab anything you want to keep."

Someone pounded on the bathroom door. I jumped.

"Jacinta? You'd like it at Miss's house. Suelita will come if we both go."

I didn't want to see Rosa. Tía told me I'd left a jagged cut across my sister's eyebrow when I punched her. If I saw her stitches, my guilt would be real. I wasn't ready to stop being the *victim.*

As Rosa shouted through the door, I crawled into the far corner of the bathtub, holding my hands over my ears. I pushed hard so the ringing in my head would drown out her voice.

When I took my hands away, the only sound I heard was cartoons. I got up and opened the door a crack. Tía swayed in the middle of the room, holding a crisp green bill.

"Miss found this money in your apartment. We can buy formula and diapers." Tía blinked, and a tear slid down her cheek.

Miss is a liar. My family wouldn't leave money lying around. She thinks she can buy us for fifty bucks.

"She brought you this," Tía said.

I wouldn't look.

The baby made a noise in the bedroom. I heard Tía's footsteps as she went to him.

My eyes strayed to find what Miss had brought. Abuelita's mirror lay on the kitchen table. It drew me like a magnet. In a heartbeat, I stood next to the table, staring down at the glass, running my fingers over it. In spite of its age and the crack across the top, it was beautiful.

No. Not in spite of it. Because of it.

How can something broken be so beautiful?

I lifted the mirror. I admired the flowers etched into the foggy silver surface. Then I caught sight of the face in the glass. My hands trembled.

In slow motion the mirror began to shake. I watched it slip from my grasp. I had all the time in the world to think. *It's going to hit the floor and shatter. Will the pieces fly up and cut me? Will it hurt?*

The glass smashed into the tiles, and splinters floated up. They looked like fish in the aquarium Miss had taken me to see, the slivers of mirror swimming through the air, then falling back.

I don't remember the sound of broken glass. Just my cousin's startled cry. The slow motion ended.

Like in a movie.

Tía rushed into the room, the baby over her shoulder. *"¿Qué pasó?"*

Staring at the pieces on the floor, I shook my head. Miss was right. My skin was perfect. But instead of flowers, my face was etched with pain.

How can someone beautiful be so broken?

29

TÍA AND I kept meaning to sneak over to my family's apartment in the dark to get some more stuff. But she'd started working nights, cleaning an office building. There never seemed to be enough time.

Her new job was good because I didn't have to skip school while she cleaned houses. Good because Tía made more money. Good because I slept in her bed while she worked, instead of on her lumpy sofa.

But it was bad because I had to put a pack of little kids to bed by myself and get up with a hungry baby every few hours. I did my sleeping at school.

Instead of reading from my *Othello* essay on jealousy, Mr. Flores gave me detention for being late to class after I dozed off at lunch. My grades were slipping, and so were my dreams of a scholarship. Everything Miss had said about college was a lie. College was for rich kids who didn't have to grow up until they were ready.

I stopped wishing for a car and a credit card. All I wanted was a nap.

It's not fair.

Then I remembered what Miss had said about fairness and grace. *What's fair for somebody who lies and scars her sister's face? What do I deserve?* A chill went through me.

Okay, God. Forget what's fair. Send grace.

But maybe God was on the other line when I called.

Every day after school, I walked by our old apartment on my way to Tía's. I was so sleepy that sometimes I forgot we didn't live there. I'd trudge down the stairwell, only to see the eviction notice on the door.

Then I'd slink away with my head down, my hair hiding my tears. Once an old neighbor lady called to me. I walked faster, pretending I didn't hear.

Then the day came when a big green garbage bin

sat in front of our old building. Two men were lifting something into its open mouth.

Our kitchen table.

My heart jumped into my throat. Our table teetered on the edge of the bin.

Then it toppled inside.

A metallic echo.

Debris flew up in a cloud.

"NO!"

I was running but not seeing. I stumbled, and the ground came up at me.

Pushing myself back on my knees, I squinted into the glare of afternoon sun. Voices around me, some familiar, some strange, asking questions, English and Spanish mixed together.

Then I saw Mr. Spitz's angry face looming over me. He held an armful of sheets and blankets. And there, right there in his arms, with the other covers from my bed, was Abuelita's afghan. The one Mamá had given me. To keep me safe.

Mine! That's mine!

I saw all his smelly brown teeth up close. "You mind telling me where your parents are?"

I stumbled to my feet and threw myself at him. As he jumped away, I grabbed the afghan and pulled. Surprised, he dropped the rest of my covers on the ground.

Then I ran, my flip-flops slapping the concrete, my backpack bouncing against my spine. Ran with Abuelita's afghan in my arms, leaving behind shrill and angry voices.

SPRING BREAK.

Like every other kid in America, I'd be glad not to go to school for a whole week. But unlike every other kid, I'd use that time for sleeping.

If I'd been lonely during Christmas, it was nothing compared to living at Tía's. I felt like the last big kid in the orphanage, surrounded by babies. Cinderella minus her fairy godmother. My life was crowded and empty at the same time.

Miss had warned me not to be alone with a boy until I was married. She was right about that. I wasn't going have a baby until I was ready.

But I didn't tell Miss that. I wasn't speaking to her. I would never speak to her again. I wouldn't wear the ring she gave me, even though I kept my promise. *Why should I wear her ring if she isn't keeping her promises?*

I missed Cody and Ethan. I missed gymnastics and ballet. I missed books and films.

But mostly I missed Mamá and Papi. They'd worked so hard to keep my sisters and me safe. But I couldn't save them.

The word for how I felt is *impotent*.

Helpless. Hopeless. Powerless.

If there's a worse feeling, I don't know what it is. I was filled with *rage*—and there wasn't one thing I could do about it. Like acid eating me from the inside—eating up all the strength that had been growing in me.

I'd thought Miss was the most honest person I'd ever met. But she turned out to be the biggest liar of all. She made me think she could do *anything*. And she made me believe *I* could be something I wasn't.

Rain washed away the snow in Maplewood, but the ice in my heart wouldn't melt.

Tía said Rosa would be going with the Dahls

to Florida for spring break. The boys' grandma was taking them all to the Magic Kingdom to see that famous cartoon mouse.

I was invited to go, too. But I refused to go anywhere with Miss.

Tía Carmen was relieved when I told her I'd *never* abandon her the way Rosa had. I didn't even want to go, I said.

Not really.

Not very much at all.

But when Tía told me the Dahls had to cancel their trip, I was glad. I knew I had meanness in me, but I didn't know I could enjoy it so much.

After spending her "last dime" on a lawyer, Miss had finally won her lawsuit with the TV station. She was going back to reading the nightly news on TV, so Rosa wasn't going anywhere. *It's only fair.*

My rage had burned down to ashes, and my smoldering anger turned inward. There's a word for that.

Depression.

And that's when I got the *final* late-night phone call.

The baby lay in my lap, almost asleep. In the glow of the television, I watched Mateo startle and start sucking again. I hoped Tía had been paid, because I'd used the last of the formula to make his bottle.

Clicking the TV remote, I looked for something on late that wasn't boring, stupid, or weird. On the third click I was stopped by a face.

Nadine Robert.

I pushed the volume button.

"—the ballet company's season finale, *Romeo and Juliet*. Good seats are still available." Then music. The sound of my own heart. Pain and loss.

Maybe Miss will take me.

But why would she, when I'm not speaking to her? Maybe she already tried to call, and I wouldn't answer. Maybe she's never going to call again.

My eyes burned. *I didn't get to ask Cody which ballet is his favorite.*

The commercial ended. The next music made my heart ache even more. 5News music.

The familiar anchor desk appeared, but this time instead of the blond lady, Miss sat next to the guy with the tie. Seeing them together, I realized he was younger than Miss.

A lot younger.

"Coming up at ten tonight, the Regional Transportation District tackles the issue of how to fund the extension of light rail."

Then Miss spoke. "And Denver water officials say we could be in for another summer drought. Rejoining Steve Barnes on the anchor desk, I'm Kathryn Dawson Dahl. 5*News Nighttime Edition* starts right after the movie."

I clicked off the television and tossed the remote onto the sofa.

A tear splashed on Mateo's cheek, startling him again. It was just as well. If I didn't burp him, we'd both be up all night.

I put his blanket over my shoulder so he wouldn't spit up on my pajamas. I lifted him slowly, then patted his back, smelling his baby hair. So tiny. A whole person, right there in my hands. *Perfect.*

Then he slid sideways. With a burp louder than a miniature person should make, a stream of baby barf rolled down my sleeve.

I sighed. *Ça ne me fait rien.* French for "It makes no difference to me."

I'd learned to lie to myself in three languages.

The phone rang.

NOW WHAT?

I didn't recognize the number, but it was long distance. I hesitated. Neither my head or my heart could take one more thing. Wincing, juggling Mateo, I reached for the phone and forced the word out of my mouth.

"*¿Bueno?*"

"*Jacinta?*"

Forgetting I had him in my arms, I squeezed Mateo and was rewarded with another spray of milky spit-up. "*¡Mamá! ¿Dónde estás?*"

Mamá didn't answer. "*Mija,* I need to speak to Carmen."

"Tía is working. Where are you?" I was practically shouting. I had to—so I could hear my voice over the sound of blood rushing around my head. Mateo started to cry.

"Rosa. Get Rosa."

I froze. "Rosa is living with Miss."

I heard her sob.

"¿Mamá? ¿Mamá, qué pasó?"

So Mamá told me. She had no choice.

A *coyote*—a paid smuggler of people—had gotten Mamá across *la línea*. Before I had time to swallow this news, to let its happiness flow through me, Mamá said the *coyote* had stolen her money while she slept in a motel, leaving her no way to pay for the room and nothing to buy a bus ticket home. She said to call Papi at his night job and tell him to come get her. Right away.

A breath. "Papi was deported."

A wail.

"Mamá?" Her cries ripped my heart. *She'll pull herself back together. Then she'll tell me what to do.* I watched Tía's digital clock tick off a minute. "Mamá?"

Still she cried.

Stunned, I held the phone away from my face. *She doesn't know! Mamá doesn't know what to do!* I felt myself drowning in the familiar sensation of helplessness. Hopelessness. *The world is a hateful, chaotic place. Bad things happen for no reason. We're pushed around by things we can't control, until we die.*

But another wave—a more powerful force—came over me. I couldn't swallow the lie. Not anymore.

My heart turned hard. Hard like a diamond.

All the strength seeping out of Mamá got sucked through the phone. Right into me. Her power, Abuelita's power, my sisters' power. The power of every woman. All of it was in me.

Even the power I thought belonged to Miss? That too.

"Mamá, no llores."

After I told her not to cry, I dumped Mateo onto the sofa next to me and shouted to Mamá over his squalling.

"Tell me where you are!" My voice. *Not* the voice of a lost little girl. The voice of someone with power. Power on the inside.

I had to repeat my words. Mamá continued crying, Mateo kept screaming. But I got what I needed and scribbled the information on the back of an envelope.

"Stay where you are, Mamá. I'm coming to get you."

"No, *mija,* I need to leave before the motel people want their money. I cannot even pay for this phone call. *La policía* will take me to jail."

"Mamá, I will bring money. You need to wait."

We argued. The time it was taking to convince her started to worry me. I imagined Miss looking at her watch. But I finally got Mamá to agree to wait for me at the motel.

Then the hard part. I didn't want to hang up. This was as close to Mamá as I'd been in months. But if I was going to rescue her, I had to do it right then, that night.

"Adiós, Mamá. Te quiero." I hung up.

And for once, I didn't cry.

Fortunately Mateo had cried himself to sleep. Careful not to wake him, I put him in his crib. Then I called Tía and told her to come home because I was going to rescue Mamá.

Tía Carmen might get fired for leaving work in the middle of the night. With no other money coming in, it was a dangerous decision. But it was what we had to do.

It's what family means.

I put my anger aside. Holding a grudge was a *luxury* I couldn't afford. Pastor Federico had said, "Forgiveness is a choice, not a feeling."

Another dangerous choice. The choice to trust again.

I took a deep breath and punched in Miss's cell phone number.

THE TIME from when the phone started ringing to when Miss picked it up was an eternity. While I waited, I practiced what I would say. I wished I could ask Miss to her face, but I didn't think my puppy-dog eyes would help.

"Carmen?" she asked.

"Miss! Mamá's back!"

"She's there? At Carmen's?"

I swallowed. "No, we need to go get her. Right now."

"What? Where?"

The blood rushed to my head, making me dizzy. "In New Mexico."

Silence.

"Miss?"

"You spent the last month hanging up on me, slamming doors in my face! Now you—you expect me to—?"

"Miss, I'm sorry. I'm really, really sorry. But I *need* you! You need to come now!"

"There's no way I can leave now! I'm about to do a newscast! Do you know how long I've waited for this?"

"She's in a motel, but her money was stolen before she could pay. We have to leave *now*! Before the police get her!"

"No. It's too dangerous," she hissed, her voiced lowered. "There's a story in the news about a guy who went to jail for driving illegals across state lines. He was just 'giving them a ride.'"

"I'm not talking about illegals! I'm talking about MAMÁ!"

She hesitated. "We'll call a lawyer tomorrow."

"MAMÁ WILL BE GONE!"

"Jacinta, I'm sorry. I've got my boys to think about."

I needed a tool.

Leverage.

So I said the one thing guaranteed to make Miss shut up.

In the silence I crossed my fingers. The digital clock flipped off another minute. I thought about saying something else, decided against it, and waited. Through the phone I felt Miss hating me.

But I hoped she'd hate herself more.

She sighed. "Give me the name of the motel."

I let out the breath I'd been holding. "I'm coming with you."

Nothing.

"I'm coming with you," I repeated.

"Bring your passport."

Miss's van coughed its way down the deserted street. In the silence of night, I could hear it long before its headlights flashed across Tía's living-room wall. I wanted to run out and hug the noisy thing. I didn't know it'd be the last trip Miss and I would make together in that van.

I ran to the front passenger side. But someone was sitting there.

"I got shotgun, small fry. You're in back," said Ethan.

I flung open the side door. The seat was empty. I was sorry not to see Cody but relieved that Rosa wasn't coming. I didn't want to see the scar I'd left on her face.

With all the politeness I could find in me, I asked, "Do you have your phone, Miss? I need to call Mamá. To tell her we're on our way, so she doesn't try to leave."

Miss handed it over.

I took the envelope with my scribbled notes out of my pocket and punched in the number for the motel.

Miss asked, "Do you want a blanket or a pillow? It's a long ride."

She was trying to be *considerate,* but I didn't want her to be nice to me. I wasn't ready to give up my anger. I *had* to forgive her, but I didn't have to *like* her.

Anyway, Mamá's sweater seemed like enough protection. Later I'd wish I'd brought Abuelita's afghan. I'd want that warmth, that security. But right then, I wanted to hurry. With the phone to my ear, I said, "No. Let's do this."

Like in the movies.

Miss snorted.

"Roger that!" said Ethan.

They were making fun of me. *Let them laugh. After tomorrow I never have to see them again.*

I must've been asleep, because I woke with a start when the van went over a bump. My feet stuck to my flip-flops where the van's heater pumped hot air under the front seat, but my back was cold and stiff.

In the glow of the dashboard, I saw the green outline of Ethan's face on the passenger side. Even though he had on headphones, I heard his music. I lay on my back and stared through the van's sunroof at the stars. They were much brighter in the New Mexico desert than in the barrio. Two of the brightest ones looked like eyes. Mamá's eyes.

"How we doing?"

Ethan's voice startled me. He'd pulled an earpiece out and was looking into his mother's face.

Miss shook her head. "I wish we knew what time checkout is."

Checkout? Would Mamá be gone before we got there? No, we won't be late. Miss is never late.

Almost never.

"You could kick it up a notch," said Ethan.

"I'm driving as fast as I dare. We can't afford to get stopped."

Then the GPS from Miss's cell phone spoke. "Take exit 339 for U.S. 84 South toward Santa Rosa."

"Mom, have you thought this through?"

"If I'd *thought* about it, would we be in the middle of nowhere at three thirty in the morning?"

I could almost hear Ethan grinning. "I get my 'impulsivity thing' from you."

Miss groaned. "Oh, God, what am I doing?"

Then she jumped, straining to look in the rear-view mirror. Voice lowered, she asked, "Is she asleep?"

I closed my eyes, hearing movement from Ethan's seat as I worked to keep my breathing steady.

He whispered, "Yeah, she's asleep."

"You should sleep. You might need to take over driving."

"I slept."

"Sleep some more."

The GPS interrupted again. "Continue on U.S. 84 South for forty-one miles."

"What happens if we get stopped with an illegal alien?" Ethan asked.

"Undocumented immigrant," she said, correcting him.

"So, what happens?"

"It's not your problem."

"Fine." But it wasn't fine. Ethan was angry. He was dealing with grown-up problems while being treated like a little kid. I knew what that felt like.

I had started to drift off to sleep again when he asked, "But—what do I do if you get arrested?"

"You didn't have to come."

"You—you think I'm worried about *me*?"

I opened my eyes a crack. He moved to put his earpiece back in, but Miss spoke. "I can't believe she lied to me."

Guilt twisted in my stomach.

Ethan snorted. She shot him a look, but he didn't flinch. "You make people lie to you."

"I *make* people lie to me?"

"You're so perfect all the time. You expect everyone to be like you."

Is he right? Is it Miss's fault I lied? I wanted to believe it.

"I'm not perfect. I know how to lie. I'm not proud of it."

"When have you ever lied?"

"Tonight. I couldn't tell Maury the real reason I was leaving. He's mad enough about being forced to put me back on the anchor desk. So I stuck my finger down my throat to make myself throw up in my trash can and went home 'sick.'"

"Great. So even if we don't get arrested, we gotta worry about you losing your job. Way to go, Mom." Ethan folded his arms and stared out his window, not looking at her.

At last Miss spoke again. "You know what she said to me? 'I broke your stupid sprinkler, and I had to make it right. Or is it just *Mexicans* who are *obligated*?'"

They turned to look at each other. I saw the green outline of her face, etched in pain. Ethan must have seen it, too. He switched off his music.

"Sure you wanna do this?" His rough voice was gentle.

"*No!* I'm *not* sure! But kids growing up without parents is—it's just wrong." Then she whispered, "Did I wake her?"

I closed my eyes before Ethan could look around. I let my mouth gape open. Drool leaked onto my arm. It tickled, but I didn't move.

"No, she's out."

"If I can fix this one thing, I'll let it go. All right?"

He snapped. "How is this *your* fault? Her dad had a busted taillight! And the 'policeman' who came to their apartment? He could've just been a truant officer! Rosa told me she'd been cutting school so the aunt could work."

My eyes popped open. *A truant officer? We skipped school that day, waiting for Papi!*

"Not so loud." Miss hushed him. "You may be right, but I'm not talking about that. It's the gymnastics. The French lessons. Pushing college on her."

"And all that's . . . bad?"

"I thought I could 'fix' her. Fix her life, anyway. How arrogant is that? Thinking I can fix her life when I can't even manage my own? I'm a—a Well-Meaning Church Lady."

"Which would make a really good name for a punk rock band."

"I'm being serious here."

"Jeez, Mom. Who died and left you in charge?"

And then Miss said the one thing that made *me* shut up.

"Jacinta would've been better off if I'd minded my own business."

The same thing I'd been thinking for weeks. But hearing it from Miss was different. Like she'd gambled her last dollar on me to win a race, and I'd let her down. Then she said, "It was a one-year commitment, okay? It's just about over. I've done enough damage."

Ethan nodded, then stuck his earpiece back in.

A small click, and I heard his music mingle with the sounds of the van on the highway.

Miss ruined my life.

She said so with her own mouth. She made it so I could never be happy with my old life, and her promise of a new life was one she couldn't keep.

Stop thinking about Miss. Focus on Mamá. Once she's back I can forget that Miss and I ever met.

32

THE VAN ROCKED as it pulled off the highway. Light streamed through the sunroof, making me blink.

Ethan yawned. "Where are we?"

"Whites City," said Miss.

I sat up.

The sun felt closer somehow, beating down on the highway, telephone poles, rocks, and dirt. The Middle of Nowhere.

Then Miss turned into the parking lot of a yellowing building with faded blue awnings. The sign read BUSY BEE MOTOR INN, but it looked like the least busy place in the world. The dog on the stoop didn't raise his head when we drove by. His eyes flicked over to the van, then closed again. He let out a breath that made his jowls flutter. Then he was still.

"Jacinta, what room's your mom in?"

I pulled the soggy envelope from the pocket of my jeans. It was sweaty from my hand gripping it through the night—to reassure myself that Mamá would be rescued. But I didn't need to unfold it.

"Seven."

Miss pulled up in front of a door. She didn't turn off the motor, which continued its *repertoire* of gurgles and moans.

"All right." She looked at me, and I realized *I* was supposed to get Mamá.

And for some reason, I was afraid.

Will Mamá even know me? Maybe she's changed, too.

My heart thumped in my ears. When I opened the van door, everything moved in slow motion. Even though it was still morning, heat coming from the pavement made the air look wavy, like in the movies.

A dream sequence.

Tar oozing from cracks in the asphalt stank and

stuck to the bottom of my flip-flops, holding me back. Mamá's sweater was sticking to my skin, but it wasn't time to take it off. Not when I was so close. I staggered around a cleaning cart to stare at the chipped blue number 7. My hand moved to the door and tapped.

Nothing.

I knocked harder.

After a million years, a voice came through the crack of the door.

"*¿Hola?*"

"*¡Mamá! ¡Soy yo!*"

The door opened. A pair of brown eyes. "*¿Sí?*"

But the woman in the maid's uniform wasn't Mamá. I struggled to breathe, but the oxygen had been sucked out of the air. I was dizzy. "*¿Dónde está mi mamá?*"

"*No sé.*"

The world grew dark.

And through the darkness, Miss's voice. "Grab her. Like this."

My face hurt. The pavement burned. I didn't know I'd fainted until I felt arms around me, hands

272

pulling on me. Miss and the stranger in the maid's uniform half carried, half dragged me back to the van.

"She okay, Miss?"

"Gracias, señora. Está bien."

Ethan's face. Reaching for me, pulling me up. Miss heaved me onto the seat with him. Cold air welcomed me. I closed my eyes.

"Is she okay?" Ethan's worried voice.

"Slide over."

"I'm driving?" I heard Ethan scramble over the hump to the other side.

"Keep the air running. I'll pay the motel bill and get some water." Miss slammed the door.

"J.J.?"

My hand moved to my throbbing temple. It was tender. I winced and pulled my hand away, blinking the world back into focus. Ethan's concerned face stared at me sideways.

This can't be right. Mamá said she would wait. Why didn't she wait?

Ethan asked my next question aloud. "Where'd your mom go?"

Slowly, testing myself, I sat up. Hammering continued on the inside of my skull. I glanced around. The hotel maid looked back over her shoulder as she pushed her cleaning cart to room 8. She gave me a tenuous wave before letting herself inside.

Ethan and I scanned the emptiness around us. *Where could she go?* Rocks and weeds baked in withering heat — it felt more like August than April.

And I knew.

I threw open the van door, my feet already moving before they touched the pavement. Around to the *back* of the crumbling motel. The *shady* side.

Still faint, I stumbled, my ankles twisting in my flip-flops, over stones and trash clinging to the clumps of dead grass.

A dented green trash bin.

"Mamá?"

The rattle of newspapers. A sun-weathered face peered from around the side of the bin. Before she could struggle to her feet, I was in her arms.

I didn't know if the tears were hers or mine, if she was shaking, or if I was. I smelled her hair. The smell wasn't flowers. It was cigarette smoke. I didn't care. I tasted her salty, wet cheek as I kissed her again and again.

She whispered, *"Mija."*

We were together. Time passed—a year, or maybe just seconds. I clung to Mamá. She was mine. I was safe. I promised myself I'd never let her go again. No matter what.

The sound of the wheezy van made Mamá startle. We turned as it rumbled around the corner, bumping over rocks and weeds—Ethan at the wheel, Miss riding shotgun.

I'd forgotten Miss and Ethan. Forgotten everything. Mamá and I scrambled to our feet, bumping into each other.

Miss climbed out and gave Mamá a weak smile. *"Hola.* Fernanda? *Vámonos, por favor."*

Mamá nodded, wiping her tears with her hands. She agreed in her little bit of English. "Yes, Miss, we go. Thank you, Miss."

Miss and Mamá acted like they knew each other, but with both of them right in front of me, I wasn't sure who I was. *Mija or mentee?*

My mentor waved me into the van, so I climbed

into the middle seat and extended my hand to Mamá. Miss closed the door behind us and jumped into the front passenger seat. "Drive."

The van belched a cloud of smoke as we lurched away.

That should have been the "Happily ever after." The part of the movie where the credits roll. What Ethan calls a Hollywood Ending.

CAPÍTULO
TREINTA Y TRES

RED LIGHT. BLUE LIGHT. The side of the patrol car said NEW MEXICO STATE POLICE. Right there on the side of the two-lane highway that had brought us here. To get home, we'd have to drive past it. At a crawl. Traffic was backed up in both directions.

My pulse throbbed in my neck. Mamá squeezed my arm.

With his hands and legs apart, a dark-skinned man leaned against the roof of a battered white pickup. An officer kept one hand on the man's back while talking into a radio attached to his shirt. Drivers craned their necks trying to get a good look. Some were even taking pictures with their cell phones.

I gulped. "Is he being arrested?"

No one answered. Mamá shrank in her seat. We hesitated in the exit of the motel parking lot, staring at the blockage in the T-intersection off to our left. Ethan's white-knuckled hands gripped the wheel.

Miss's voice was calm. "Just turn left."

The car rolled forward and turned. To the right.

"Left! I said left!"

"Really? You wanted me to drive *into* that mess?" Ethan asked.

"We've got to. Turn around," Miss ordered.

Mamá's violent trembling made me afraid. I didn't want to drive by a squad car and that man getting arrested. "No, Miss! This road will come out somewhere, won't it?"

Ethan continued to roll away from the flashing lights. A siren screamed behind us. Miss, Mamá, and I whipped around to see a second patrol car edge around the highway traffic on the shoulder.

I looked ahead to see Ethan crane his neck, checking the rearview mirror.

"*Mom?*" Not his usual voice. The voice of a little kid.

Concern flickered across Miss's face. After a pause, she said to Ethan, "Okay. Just drive."

Relieved, I told Mamá, "We're going to find another way home."

Mamá breathed, "Thank you, Miss."

Her normally soft skin was rough and leathery—parched and peeling—and almost as dark as mine. The yellowing shadow of a bruise lingered on her cheek, just below her eye. Her lips were purplish black and cracked.

I didn't recognize the ripped and grimy pants and shirt she wore. They hung on her, just as the skin seem to hang on her bones. There wasn't enough of her to fill them out.

Cuts covered her arms. Another cut on her neck oozed, as if it wasn't healing just right. *Had she been this beat up when she returned from Mexico the last time?* I couldn't remember. I wanted to find the people who'd done this to her and show them I knew how to use a baseball bat.

But Mamá was the whole world, right there in my arms. Safe. After more than a year, I was finally safe.

She kissed my forehead over and over. Angel kisses.

Miss watched from the front seat with a small, sad smile.

It was too much.

Tears burst out. *Happy, sad, angry, afraid. Too much. Too, too much. A swirl of Mamá's and Miss's faces.* I squeezed my eyes shut, but the flood kept coming. *My heart. So full, exploding. My mouth, open and gasping. Air, I need air.*

Mamá's arms tightened around me. Her worried voice traveled through my haze. "Jacinta?"

Then Miss. "Jacinta!"

No, don't! Don't say it. Whatever it is, don't say it. I can't think. I can't breathe. Please, please, don't say anything.

"Drink this, or you're going to get a headache."

I opened my eyes a crack. Miss held out a bottle of water.

Oh. Okay.

Mamá brushed my hair away from my face, soothing the ragged edges of my nerves, as the water bathed my raw throat. I drained the bottle.

Then I struggled out of Mamá's sweater. She helped pull it off me. I thought she might ask why I wore the filthy thing, but she said nothing and dropped it on the floor of the van. I felt silly for all the times I'd insisted on wearing it. But the charm had worked. Mamá was back.

Her eyes darted from Miss to me. The three of us exchanged looks.

Miss must have realized she was staring at something private. She blushed and turned to face forward. She asked Ethan, "Where are we?"

"You said, 'Drive.' I drove."

Miss pulled her phone from its holder, looked at it, then groaned. "The battery's dead."

"Use the car charger."

"The lighter doesn't work. The van's electrical system is shot."

Ethan sighed. "You should've bought *me* a smartphone. At least then we'd still have GPS."

"Does it occur to you that we're living on one

income? That we can no longer buy whatever our little hearts desire?"

"Did we ever?" Ethan steered the van around winding curves.

We were on a twisting road. Wildflowers, cactuses, and other plants dotted the landscape. It was kinda pretty, but not familiar.

"Should I—? Do I—? You want me to turn around?" he asked.

"Not here. It's too dangerous."

I glanced around. A line of cars snaked behind us. *What are all these people doing here?* I faced forward—just as we passed the sign.

"Oh, my goodness," said Miss.

"Oh, wow!" said Ethan.

Mamá asked in Spanish, "What did the sign say, *mija?*"

"No sé," I told her. Then we were in a parking lot. *A parking lot in the Middle of Nowhere?* A man in a uniform, wearing a badge, waved Ethan into a space.

Mamá gripped my arm.

"Miss, where are we?"

"What should I do?" asked Ethan.

"Go ahead and park."

He moved to pull into a space, but Ethan was new to parking. It looked like he might hit the car next to us. Miss shouted, "Crank your wheel!"

He slammed on the brakes instead. We lurched forward in our seats. The man in the uniform got that "patient" look on his face.

I tried to hang on to Mamá, feeling her panic, but she slipped to the floor, cowering behind Miss's seat.

"What is this place?" I asked again.

Miss pulled her eyes from the parking space while Ethan eased the van forward. She looked from me to Mamá. A gentle smile broke through Miss's look of concern. She touched Mamá's hand.

"Está bien, está bien," said Miss.

"Where *are* we?" I insisted as Ethan switched off the engine.

Miss's eyes sparkled. "Tell your mom we're in Fairyland."

WHEN ETHAN SAID we were at Carlsbad Caverns National Park, the words meant nothing to me. But he was excited. "Mom, can we go inside the cave?"

"No, I'm supposed to anchor the show tonight."

"Stick your finger down your throat and tell them you're still vomiting."

Miss glanced at me, to see if I was listening. She lowered her voice and said to Ethan, "It's still lying."

"No, it isn't."

They argued across the parking lot, up to the visitor center. I practically had to drag Mamá, reassuring her as Miss had, *"Está bien, está bien."*

Mamá's eyes darted to the park ranger directing traffic. To his uniform.

I called out to Miss, "Can't we just go?"

"I need to use the restroom," she shouted over her shoulder.

Since I'd chugged a whole bottle of water, a bathroom break seemed like a good idea. Even if yelling it all over the parking lot wasn't. I whispered to Mamá, *"El baño."*

She stopped resisting.

An older lady in the women's room stared at Mamá. At her wounds.

"Rough trail," I told the lady.

She nodded and backed out the door. I imagined her running to the cashier, trying to get her money back.

I helped Mamá clean up a bit, lending her my hairbrush.

Miss looked almost as bad, in her own way. She glanced in the mirror and started digging around in her purse as Mamá and I left the bathroom.

Ethan grabbed my arm. "This is perfect."

"What's perfect?"

"This place! This is our alibi! If we get stopped by police on the way home, we say we came for spring break! We'll have the tickets to prove it!"

"But this place scares Mamá."

"There's only one road in or out. We'll have to drive by those cops if we leave now. Don't you wanna see the cave?"

And I realized I did. I wanted this *educational opportunity*. Who knew when I might have another chance? Miss's year as my mentor was nearly over.

And I'd just spent nine hours in her stupid van.

Miss emerged from the ladies' room looking more like her regular self.

"Are we going in?" Ethan asked her again.

"I told you, I need to get back to my job."

Ethan whined. "Even if we left this minute, you'd never make it for the five o'clock show. And we're hungry. There's a cafeteria inside the cave."

Mamá looked from Ethan to Miss. "What are they saying?"

"Ethan says there's a restaurant inside the cave."

Mamá shook her head. "No, we need to go home."

Miss frowned. "What did your mom say?"

I wound my hair around a finger. "She hasn't had anything to eat today."

Using Ethan's disposable phone, I called Rosa. I wanted to be the one to say we'd rescued Mamá. Rosa was so excited that she couldn't stop shouting. After she talked to Mamá, I got back on the line and told her to call Tía. I'd wanted to tell my aunt myself, but Miss said we needed to save Ethan's phone battery since we didn't have the charger for it.

Ethan and I ran ahead on the trail, to look into the gaping mouth of the enormous cave. Staring down into it, little bumps popped out on my arms, despite the hot dry air. I stepped away from the stone wall. It felt like I might fall in. Mamá walked up behind me, then gripped my arm with both hands.

Even with a spring break crowd descending into the massive opening, we felt like the only ones there. The cave is that *majestic*. That *awesome*.

Once again, Miss was right. *Awesome* is a word to save for when you need it.

You might think people would shout inside a big cave to hear the echo. That didn't happen. The horde of people approaching that emptiness made almost no noise. As if none of us wanted to wake the sleeping beast and get swallowed in one gulp. Maybe we'd all watched the same kids' movie, where the guy is trapped in a cave of wonders and finds a genie.

I looked at Mamá and was surprised to see that I was taller than she was. It shocked me again, to see her cuts and bruises. "How'd you get so beat up?"

She shook her head and wouldn't look at me. "It is not for little ears."

At the word *little,* I pulled her around to stare down at her. My glaze slipped past her eyes, into her soul. *Pain. Too much pain.*

I looked away, feeling sick.

Who did this to her? Vigilantes? Americans who try to stop illegals from crossing? Or was it Mamá's own coyote *who hurt her?* I'd never know. Mamá wasn't going to tell me. And I could never bear to hear.

Rage. Impotence.

I wanted to punish Mamá for allowing herself

to get hurt. For what her scars were doing to *me*. For leaving me for more than a *year*. I thought about walking with Miss, rubbing it in Mamá's face while I held Miss's hand, my pinkie wrapped around her finger.

But I was angry with Miss, too. She was leaving me. *No. I'm leaving her.*

I shoved my hands in my pockets and walked by myself down the zigzag trail.

But as I moved into the darkness, Carlsbad proved it *was* a cave of wonders. Nature had carved gardens and castles, animals and faces, out of the rock. I glided past unchanging worlds. Cold, restless air whispered stories I could almost understand.

I felt my anger slipping, so I tried to pull it tight around me. Like a *shroud.*

But in all that peace, my rage came unraveled and fell from my shoulders in rags. As I moved along the maze of trails, my mind worked through the *labyrinth* of my own thoughts.

Why do I pull away from the people I love? It's kinda stupid.

No. It's REALLY stupid.

Because what I want—what I really want—is to be close.

My hand moved out of my pocket, searching. And found Mamá's warm, rough one. I thought we'd come to the caverns by accident. A wrong turn. But maybe there's no such thing as coincidence. Maybe there's a *plan.*

Is this grace?

THE DRIVE FROM Carlsbad Caverns to Roswell took two hours. Two long, boring hours. I was glad I'd slept the first time we drove through it. But Ethan was excited. As we rolled into town, he said, "Keep your eyes peeled for aliens!"

He didn't mean undocumented immigrants. He meant creatures from another planet. He told me that Roswell is the Unidentified Flying Object capital of the world.

When we stopped at a gas station, Ethan warned me that the town has a reputation for otherworldly phenomena. He was right, because when he asked Miss for soda, she said, "Only if it has caffeine."

"Who are you, and what've you done with my mother?"

"You'll need it. You're driving."

"Great." But he meant the opposite.

Miss was beyond tired. She hadn't slept the night before. Ethan and I had dozed during the long ride, but Miss had stopped only for gasoline, coffee, and to use the ladies' room. Her hair was greasy and clung to her face. She looked old. *Old enough to be my* abuelita.

But I thought about the wrong turn Ethan made leaving the motel parking lot—the one that brought us to Carlsbad Caverns. *Is it a good idea to have a resentful, inexperienced teenager with ADD driving with an illegal in the car?*

Then I got mad at myself for thinking that. *How can a person be "illegal"? How can Mamá be illegal?*

When we opened the doors to climb back into the van, hot air pushed out at us. We didn't want to get back into that "sauna on wheels," as Ethan called it.

Miss ordered him into the driver's seat. She sat in front next to him, but handed *me* the map she'd bought, since we didn't have GPS. The sweat on my lip wasn't only from the heat. I was nervous about being the *navigator*. But I was happy, too. Mamá would see how much I'd learned.

When the time came, I'd be the driver for our family, so Papi wouldn't have to risk being deported again—if we could track down his truck and get it back. *I won't be a scaredy-cat driver like Ethan.*

With a cough and a sputter, the van shook itself. Ethan cranked the air conditioner all the way up, but Miss turned it down again. "You want this thing to overheat?"

We inched across the parking lot.

"Which way?" Ethan asked.

I unfolded the map.

Miss leaned slowly forward, like it hurt. She tapped on the windshield with her left hand. She wasn't taking any more chances that Ethan would turn the wrong way.

When there were no cars in either direction for several blocks, Ethan rolled the van forward and turned left onto the main street.

"*Duerma*, Miss," said Mamá.

"She says you should get some sleep."

Miss gave Mamá a tired smile. "*Gracias,*

Fernanda. I need to stay awake. Ethan only has a learner's permit."

I translated.

As Ethan relaxed, we picked up speed. Not that he'd win any racing trophies. I was urging him on in my head, wishing he could be a bit braver.

The road left Roswell and became a highway stretching across emptiness. Within a minute, Miss's head lolled back. Her mouth hung open, and she snored. In a ladylike way.

Ethan leaned forward and turned up the air-conditioning. I could've kissed him. What Miss had said about "overheating" didn't make sense. *How can cold air make the van too hot?*

Mamá and I talked quietly. She cried when I told her we'd been evicted. I reminded her that things can be replaced, that we could live with Carmen until Papi got back.

I didn't say that Papi might not come back. But she knew. She stared out the window, her face turned away, her hand moving to wipe her eyes. I rubbed her shoulder. I didn't feel like the daughter.

After several minutes, Mamá asked me to tell

her more about Miss. So I started explaining all about my mentor.

But I ended up talking about me.

I could see in Mamá's eyes that she was proud of me. Proud of my knowledge of French and ballet and film. Proud of my gymnastics. Mostly, she was proud of my love of books. It was more than knowing how to read. I'd become *literate*.

Hearing the story in my own voice, I finally understood. The story of Miss wasn't about being famous or the stuff she bought me. It wasn't even about her clumsy attempts to "save" me. It was all about the time she gave to me.

She thought that I was worth it.

And I realized that I was.

The next town on the map was Las Vegas. I was excited until Ethan explained that it wasn't the *real* Las Vegas. The real Las Vegas is in Nevada.

Ethan told me he was going to move to the real Las Vegas someday and become a stage magician. I asked how that would work with him being a film director.

He didn't answer.

Miss woke when we stopped to use the bathroom in the fake Las Vegas. She started scolding us for letting her fall asleep, but she stopped when Ethan opened the door to get out.

"Uh-oh," they said together.

Then I smelled it, too. *Burning.* Mamá pointed to the wisps rising from the front of the van.

"Pop the top," Miss ordered.

Ethan did. She used the edge of her blouse to protect her hand as she pushed open the hood, leaving an oily smudge on her clothes that would never come out. Smoke billowed.

Ethan and I got out to look.

"Don't step in that," said Miss. A small greenish puddle at my feet.

Miss went inside to buy drinks for us and *coolant* for the car. She showed me and Ethan where in the engine to pour the thick green liquid.

Ethan muttered, "Car trouble as an 'educational opportunity.'"

When we got back in the van, Miss had him roll

down the windows. Then she made him turn on the *heater*.

"Why? It's hotter than hell!"

"Don't swear. The fan will blow the hot air out of the engine."

"Yeah, right into my face!"

"Life's hard. Don't let me fall asleep."

But once we were back on the highway, she started snoring again. Her coffee was left to grow cold in the cup holder.

"Shouldn't you wake her up?" I asked Ethan.

"I'm not that brave. Knock yourself out."

I decided I wasn't that brave, either.

Pretty soon Mamá slept, too. Her head rested on my shoulder, which was nice until my arm starting sweating. Then it went numb.

And I had to squint. Hot air from the heating vents and the open windows—full of grit and nasty car smells—blew into my face.

How can we still be in New Mexico? I remembered the time I'd thought Miss had kidnapped Rosa and me and taken us across state lines.

"Ethan, where's Phoenix?" I tried to yell *quietly* over the sounds of the wind and the road, not wanting to wake Miss or Mamá.

He shouted back over his shoulder. "It's — east — no, west. In Arizona. The next state over."

How ridiculous I'd been all those months ago. Thinking we'd driven through two other states when we hadn't even left Maplewood. Miss's words came back to me. "Your world is too small."

On the map, Colorado and New Mexico were on different sides of the paper. We'd been looking at rocks and weeds all afternoon and still had hours to go.

Wiping wetness from my face with my free hand, I remembered how much I hated that van. I needed a cold drink and a bathroom. I needed air that didn't smell like a pan left on the burner too long.

Anything would be better than this.

36

ALMOST TWO HOURS after our stop in the fake Las Vegas, I saw the green sign with white letters. Another town. Ethan and I were the only ones awake.

My stomach grumbled, reminding me it'd been hours since we ate at Carlsbad Caverns.

And I had to pee.

"Are you hungry?" I asked.

"Kinda."

"Let's stop."

"I—I don't know."

"If we don't eat now, we'll have to wait until we get to Colorado." I didn't mention we were ten minutes from the Colorado border.

Ethan pulled off the highway onto the main street through town.

"Should we —? You want to wake Mom?" he asked.

Probably Miss would have agreed it was dinner-time. But I couldn't be sure. I was cranky, tired, and hungry. And I had to pee. "She gave me the map, remember? I'm in charge."

Ethan snorted. We rolled slowly past several restaurants.

"*Pick* a place," I urged.

"I'm driving. *You* pick a place."

"You can't *drive* and *look* at the same time?"

"I'd like to see you try it," he muttered.

"You drive like an old lady."

Ethan pushed down on the pedal. My head jerked backward. "Now you're going too fast! How am I supposed to pick a restaurant?"

"Not so easy, is it?"

Our mothers started to wake up. I didn't want them to veto my plan. I wanted dinner, and I had to pee. "There's a place! TURN! *TURN RIGHT HERE!*"

I really did mean turn *right*.

But I was behind him, so Ethan couldn't see where I pointed.

And Ethan gets his right and left mixed up.

He yanked the steering wheel hard to the left.

Left, across two sets of double yellow lines.

Left, in front of oncoming traffic.

Left, to blaring horns.

A hard left into a *U-turn.* On two wheels.

I was thrown right. The last thing I saw was the coffee cup flying through the air.

Then my head struck Mamá's jaw. I winced in pain, seeing stars. Mamá moaned. Burning rubber, squealing tires. I braced myself.

A siren. I opened my eyes a crack. Colored lights, blue and red, flashed across the roof of the van and the back of Ethan's head.

He slammed on the brakes. Mamá and I were thrown forward. The van pulled to the right and bounced to a stop against the curb. I was tossed like a cloth doll.

The siren stopped.

I pushed myself back in my seat, rubbing my

head. I looked at Mamá. Her chin was red, her lip broken open and bleeding.

Ethan looked over his shoulder. Colored lights flashed on the side of his face.

Miss whipped around, her face glowing red, then blue, then red again. "Oh, God."

I turned.

Red light, blue light.

Waves of heat from the street blurred the edges of the car behind us. I squinted, and an apparition from my nightmares emerged. The uniformed man with the badge. In the glare of late-afternoon sun, the watery figure moved toward us.

This isn't happening. This can't be happening.

Mamá moaned again, melting behind the seat. Miss looked at me, her mouth moving. Her words swam through the air, reaching my mind. "Sit up! Tell her to sit up!"

"Sit up," I told Mamá in Spanish. My voice sounded far away. My ears were ringing.

I had to pee.

A shadow fell across Mamá's face. I turned. He

passed my window. Not all of him—I couldn't see the top of his head. His gun was below eye level.

"Afternoon, young man. I'll need your license, registration, and proof of insurance." Even his voice wore a badge.

"My son's only got a learner's permit." Miss's clear, familiar voice was gone. She sounded like a squeak toy.

"Then I'll need to see your license, too, ma'am."

Miss fumbled in the glove compartment, then her purse. Ethan struggled to get his wallet out of his back pocket.

Mamá squeezed my hand. My ruby ring cut into my finger. I remembered slipping it on before Miss came to pick me up at Tía's apartment.

Was it just last night?

The documents were handed through the window. The man in the uniform shuffled through them. "You're from Colorado? Enjoying your stay in the Land of Enchantment?"

New Mexico was more like the Land of Perpetual

Sweat, but I didn't say so. I couldn't have spoken if my life depended on it.

"We've been to Carlsbad Caverns. For spring break." Miss sounded like the cartoon mouse after he'd sucked on a helium balloon.

"I'll ask you to wait," the other voice said. I watched through the window as his badge passed under my nose.

The next second I was hit by questions from Mamá.

Miss snapped at her, "No Spanish!" Then she said to me, "No English, either!" She turned to Ethan. *"What happened?"*

"She told me to turn."

"You take orders from a twelve-year-old?"

"You gave her the map!"

Miss glanced at the patrol car behind us. "Does he know I was sleeping?"

Ethan snorted. "How should I know? I'm a sixteen-year-old."

"Let me do the talking. Unless he asks you a direct question. If you don't know, just say so. Don't guess. And don't lie."

"Whatever."

My mind scrambled to find a way out. "Miss! Show him our tickets from Carlsbad Caverns. That's our alibi."

"I'll handle this," Miss snapped. She gave Mamá a tissue for her lip. Then we waited. And waited.

I really needed to pee.

Is the officer being slow on purpose? To torture us?

Miss had said that *thinking* and *adrenaline* are a bad mix. Fight or flight. Definitely *flight*. Running down the street screaming seemed like a good idea.

"Should I tell him I have my passport, Miss?"

"No Spanish, no English!" she hissed again.

There's a solution, I thought in disgust. *What's taking so long? What if he arrests Mamá? What if he takes Miss and Ethan, too? What will happen to me? Foster care? I didn't even say good-bye to my sisters. If I hadn't insisted we stop. If I hadn't gotten into that stupid fight with Ethan. If I hadn't been so hot and tired and hungry.*

My heart was a bird, beating against my rib cage, trying to escape.

Mamá's face was a mask of fear. I wiped my

sweaty hand—the one she wasn't squeezing—on my pants and tried to think.

No Spanish, no English. A lot of help that is.

Miss had shown me that the only power was in *words*. Now she wanted me to be silent while my life slipped away.

Again.

This time, I knew there were things Miss couldn't fix.

If there were a perfume called Fear, we could've made a lot of money. Ethan pumped out gallons of it, watching his side mirror. I saw him stiffen, then the shadow of the man in the uniform fell across me.

The officer leaned in the window. I could see my own face distorted in his sunglasses.

"Son, do you know why I stopped you today?"

Ethan looked at his hands on the wheel. "Because—ah—because back there—I shouldn't have made a U-turn back there?"

He gulped and licked his lips.

"You know what double-double yellow lines mean?" the officer asked.

"You're not allowed to — not supposed to — it means you can't drive over it?"

I started to relax. Maybe this wasn't my fight. Maybe that's why Miss said what she said. Maybe this was between the police officer and Ethan.

"Those laws keep you safe." The officer handed Ethan a piece of paper and a pen. "I'm going to let you off with a warning. You need to sign it."

Ethan signed, then handed the paper and pen back to the officer, who tore off a copy of the paper and gave it to Ethan. "You folks have a safe drive home."

A pause between fear and relief. One deep breath.

But in that moment the man with the badge turned his head to include Mamá and me, sitting behind Ethan. The beginnings of a smile froze on his face. Looking into the twin mirrors of his sunglasses, I saw Mamá sitting next to me. I saw what the officer saw. Looking into Mamá's eyes, I could see her soul.

Not just fear.

Guilt.

"WHERE'D you folks say you've been?" The officer's voice had a new edge to it.

The fight-or-flight response. The only thing keeping me from doing either one was the adrenaline clogging my system.

Miss spoke in that squeak that didn't belong to her. "Carlsbad Caverns. I have the receipts right here, Officer."

I winced. It was the truth, but it wasn't the whole truth. Miss knew it, and now the policeman knew it, too.

"I need you folks to step out of the vehicle."

A new surge of adrenaline tipped the balance. Fight mode. Snatching my purse, I slid open the door and hurled myself at the man, grabbing his arm. *"S'il vous plaît, monsieur! S'il vous plaît!"*

He threw off my hand, stumbling back. *"WHAT THE —?"*

His sunglasses hit the asphalt.

I staggered forward, stepping on the lenses, shattering them. *"Je vous en prie, monsieur! Je vous en prie!"*

His hand moved to his hip. Cars swerved around him. I fumbled to open my purse.

I heard the snap pop open on his holster.

"Drop the bag!"

My hand scrambled around inside my purse, trying to find my passport.

He pointed his gun. At me.

In the van behind me, Mamá screamed.

I froze. My hair stood away from my scalp. *Would he really shoot me?*

"DROP THE PURSE! DO IT NOW!"

A memory flashed through my mind. Miss dumping the packet of trail mix out of her purse at the basketball game.

Slowly I withdrew my empty hand, then tipped

my purse upside down. In slow motion, pens, pencils, nail polish, lip gloss, and my hair brush fell, then bounced across the street in all directions. Into the paths of oncoming cars.

Brakes squealed. Horns blared. Traffic came to a stop.

I dropped the purse.

"Jacinta! What are you doing?"

The corner of my eye caught movement. I turned to look.

Miss ran around the front of the van.

The officer shouted, "STOP!"

She stopped.

Then I saw that Mamá had jumped out of the van, too.

Turning back, I looked into the officer's eyes — and saw his *indecision*.

He didn't know where to point the gun.

My eyes scanned the asphalt for my passport. Spying it, I fell to my knees.

The officer jumped. His aim followed me.

People flowed out of buildings, craning to see over each other. Drivers leaned out of their windows.

I snatched up my passport.

The officer braced himself.

Holding out the blue booklet, I pleaded, *"Allez, monsieur, regardez! Vous voyez? Je suis américaine, monsieur! S'il vous plaît, laissez-moi tranquille!"*

The policeman stood in the center of a crowd, his gun pointed at me as I groveled on the pavement. Sweat soaked the armpits of his shirt as he gaped.

Slowly he lowered his gun.

"What's she saying?" he croaked. His eyes never left me, but everyone else looked at Miss.

So did I.

She blinked. Then she spoke.

Spoke in her TV voice so everyone would hear. "She says she's an American, and she begs you to leave her in peace."

Her explanation did nothing to clear the confusion on the officer's face. People murmured. His eyes finally took in the crowd around us. His face was deep red and sweaty as he returned his gun to its holster.

Someone might wonder, *What was Jacinta thinking?* But that's just it. I *wasn't* thinking. For the first time, Miss was wrong. Thinking and adrenaline aren't a *bad* mix. They *don't* mix.

The officer strode over to Miss. Lowering his voice, he bit off each word. *"Get—her—things—and—get—back—in—the—car."*

He snatched his broken sunglasses off the street, then barked to the crowd, "Move along! It's over! Clear the area!"

Some people looked relieved. Others seemed disappointed as they shoved their phones back into their pockets. The officer directed traffic around us while Miss gathered my stuff. I stood on shaking legs, my knees burned and bleeding from the blistering asphalt. I stumbled to the van.

Mamá grabbed me and dragged me back inside with her. She hugged me to her, her face wet with tears. I whispered for her to stay quiet, but she sobbed, trembling.

Miss dumped my stuff on the seat next to me and slammed the door closed. Then she waved Ethan over.

He leaped gratefully into the passenger seat. She

climbed in the driver side, grabbing the wheel for support, her hands shaking.

The policeman slammed the door behind her and leaned into Miss's window. His heavy breath blew strands of her oily hair. She leaned away. His face was an angry shade of purple.

He glared at me. Still clipping his words, he asked Miss, "What—did she think—I was going to do?"

"Sh-she's seen people get deported. She wanted you to know that she belongs here."

"*Et ma mère aussi. Il faut qu'elle reste chez moi,*" I said.

"And her mother, too." Miss didn't translate the last part, that I needed Mamá with me. But it was true.

The officer continued to glower at me, his face a mix of embarrassment and resentment for what I'd put him through, causing him to hold a gun on a kid in front of a crowd.

This isn't such a big town. Everybody's going to hear about this.

There's a word for what I felt. *Remorse.*

313

"Je m'excuse, monsieur. Désolée."

His face told me that he understood it was an apology. He asked Miss, "What language is that? French? Her family's from French Guiana?"

Miss shifted in her seat. "One of those places south of here."

Even when she wasn't exactly lying, Miss was a bad liar.

He gave me a piercing look. I almost dropped my eyes again.

That would've been a mistake.

It would've been so easy to let my eyes slip away from his. But everything I'd learned in the past year argued against it. It was time to claim my power. My *Jacinta Juárez* power.

Without his sunglasses, I could see into his soul. His eyes said he was trying to decide what to do with me. Jerking his head in my direction, he asked Miss, "She a good student?"

There was surprise in her voice, but otherwise Miss sounded like herself. "Quite gifted, actually."

Gifted? The word flared in my mind, like a newly lit birthday candle.

I lifted my chin a bit more and allowed the man in the uniform—the stranger with the gun and the handcuffs—to look right into my eyes. Not my puppy-dog eyes.

I let him see my soul.

Let him see my pain. Let him read my love for my family. Let him see my need to belong, to feel safe. To hang on to those who belonged to me.

It wasn't a demand for fairness. It was an *appeal* for *grace*.

I made myself vulnerable, but whatever he decided, I would carry my power inside.

His look traveled across Mamá's trembling form, but he made his eyes soft, trying not to hurt her with a rough stare. Light came into his eyes as he read the story in her sun-ravaged, beaten body. A hoarse whisper. "*¿Su madre es mejicana?*"

A cold thrill went through me. I felt Mamá stiffen when he asked in Spanish if she was Mexican.

But the time for lies and manipulation was past. We'd seen into each other's souls.

My head tilted up, then down. The smallest of movements.

After a few moments—or maybe a lifetime— his eyes slid away from mine. He looked at Miss. "Your little friend has made a big problem for me. I could lose my job over this."

I sensed her tension as she waited to learn what he would do.

But I already knew.

He said, "You have exactly ten minutes to get back to Colorado."

"WHAT the *HELL* was *THAT*?"

Miss was shouting at me as the van barreled through town. She wasn't exactly speeding, but she wasn't wasting any of our ten minutes, either. I opened my mouth to say something, but Miss wasn't through.

"You could have been killed! You don't go grabbing a cop! What were you thinking?" Again I started to answer her, but it was a rhetorical question. "Never mind! You *weren't* thinking! Of all the stupid tricks!"

Mamá started yelling, too, her face dripping with sweat and tears. Almost the same words, but in Spanish. I was bawled out in two languages.

Stereo.

Ethan glanced over his shoulder at me. I thought he'd be mad, too.

But he winked! I dropped my eyes and pressed my lips together to keep from laughing, while Miss and Mamá harangued me.

They were still taking turns telling me off when we passed the sign that read, WELCOME TO COLORFUL COLORADO. Even when they'd finished, they sat there breathing hard. The lecture continued in their twin sets of glaring eyes.

I shrugged. "You said, 'No English, no Spanish.'"

Miss opened her mouth. Strange noises pushed past her lips. It took me a few moments to recognize them. *She's laughing?* Wild, hysterical laughter. Then the shrill sounds changed to her airy, snorting laugh.

Ethan cackled.

We couldn't help it. Mamá and I joined them. If it were possible for a van to explode from *hilarity,* we would've been blown to bits.

We pulled off at the first town we came to.

Neither Miss nor Ethan was fit to drive. We were tired, we were shaken. We were starving.

And I still had to pee.

Miss was outside the restaurant using Ethan's phone to call her work when our dinners arrived. I wanted her to hurry. I knew how she felt about her food getting cold, and I didn't want her to send it back when Mamá was with us. I didn't need her making a *scene*.

As the server put my plate of lasagna in front of me, the spicy aroma made my stomach growl. So I was too busy eating to study Miss's face when she came back inside. But I did notice that her grease-smeared shirt was stained with coffee. Her hair was a wreck, and her makeup was seeping into the wrinkles around her eyes. My famous mentor was a spectacular mess.

But no one gave her a second look. *Maybe her TV show airs only around Denver? Her world is too small!*

She slid into the booth next to Ethan. I was

telling Mamá that Cody had taught me to make lasagna, so I wasn't paying much attention to Miss. I'd just thought she was having one of her messy moments. Until I heard Ethan's voice.

"Mom?"

Then I really looked at her. And I knew.

"They fired you," Ethan said. It wasn't a question.

Someone who didn't know him might think he was angry, but I knew better. Ethan was afraid.

Miss blinked several times, pushing back the water in her eyes. Her voice was low when she said to Ethan, "We'll discuss this later."

She eyed the poached salmon on her plate, then looked away. As though she might be sick. Her food had grown cold, but she didn't send it back.

She didn't eat it, either.

Suddenly the smell of my lasagna made me gag.

Mamá noticed I'd stopped eating. She glanced around and saw that Miss and Ethan weren't eating, either. I was about to tell her Miss had been fired.

Miss spoke. "Don't."

I played with my hair as I mumbled to Mamá that everyone was too tired to eat.

Miss wadded up her napkin. "Let's not rush home. We'll get a couple of rooms and start again in the morning."

She said we'd call Rosa and let her know to get her stuff packed. We'd pick her up around noon the next day, then Miss would drop the three of us off at Tía's house.

And that would be that.

There were two beds in the hotel room I shared with Mamá, but I crawled under the covers with her. I needed to know I could reach for her and she'd be there. We left the bathroom light on, in case we had to get up in the night. I could see the outline of Mamá's face, her warm curves. I watched her sleep, trying to convince myself she'd really come back.

I wanted it to be true, but I knew. Some part of her hadn't returned—would never return. A piece of her soul had been ripped away. I imagined it hanging on the barbed wire of *la línea*.

I lay on my back while tears rolled down the sides of my face, into my ears.

* * *

As slowly as our trip the day before had passed, the next morning slipped away as we drove through the dull brown landscape. The air grew cold. A forgiving blanket of snow softened the sharp edges of the jagged purple mountains to the west.

Miss had never been mine. She'd been on loan to me, like a book from the library. Her year as my mentor was over. I'd wasted precious weeks of it refusing to speak to her.

And far worse, Mamá was lost to me, too. The best I could do was form a new bond with the frightened soul who'd replaced her. And Mamá would be living with a stranger who looked something like her daughter but wasn't the same person as the girl she'd left.

The green beast prowled in its dungeon. I felt greedy and mean, and guilty for feeling that way. I wanted the *old* Mamá *and* Miss. I wanted them both. But I couldn't have either one.

"*¿Tienes sueño?*" Mamá asked me.

I told her I hadn't slept well because I was excited to have her back.

She gave me a shadow of her old smile. I snuggled against her.

It's enough.

We pulled over one last time for gas and coffee in Colorado Springs, less than an hour south of Maplewood. Miss bought more coolant and wanted me to pour it into the engine. *My final educational opportunity.*

I paused. I set the bottle of coolant down on the curb and pulled off my ruby ring. "I think you should have this."

Miss didn't reach for it. Pain moved across her face. "I know — it wasn't my place to give you that ring."

"No, Miss! I just meant — you can sell it and get the money."

I was surprised to see her smirk crawl up one side of her face. "Don't worry about it. I'm rich, remember?"

I hung my head. "But it's my fault you lost your job."

Her smile disappeared. "No. You mustn't think that. I'm responsible for my decisions."

"What are you going to do?"

The lopsided grin came back. "What I should've done a long time ago. Sell that monstrosity of a house and use the money to go after some child support."

"So—you're happy about it?" I asked hopefully.

"Not exactly. But I'll figure it out." She leaned over and picked up the bottle of coolant. "Now, pour."

The green goop started leaking out of the engine even before we got back in the van. Looking at the slimy puddle on the ground made me queasy.

Ethan had crawled into the backseat to sleep. Mamá asked if I would sit up front with Miss so she could lie down on the middle seat.

I nodded, glad for the chance to say what needed to be said.

But once the van hiccuped onto the freeway, my brain stopped working. Miss had taught me hundreds of words—my mind sifted through them—but nothing seemed right. I tried not to worry about saying the perfect thing.

Just say something. ANYTHING.

Miles and minutes slipped by. The lump in my throat became an ache. I knew what I wanted to say. Magic words, spoken in the *future tense*. Words that could make us *amigas*—spelled with a small *a*.

Friends.

I didn't want to be Miss's charity work. I didn't want her to feel *obligated* or as though it was her job to rescue me. I wanted to be the kind of friend to Miss that I should've been to Angélica. Someone who can give and take, and never keep score.

But Miss's year as my mentor was up. I'd heard her tell Ethan. The only words left to say were all in the *past* tense.

As though hearing my thoughts, Miss turned, her eyes filling. Magically, the words came. They hung softly in the air between us.

"Thanks for everything. I'm sorry for the mess I made. But I'm glad that—that I got to know you."

All the right words.

But I wasn't the one who'd said them.

With her eyes still on the road, Miss held out her hand. I took it, then wrapped my pinkie around her index finger.

I think she understood.

DÉJÀ VU. It means "already seen" in French. That's how it felt, driving through the white neighborhood to the Dahl house. As though it had all happened before. I kept turning around to see Mamá stretched out on the seat behind me. It was real. We'd saved her.

Saved pieces of her.

How can she sleep? The metal-on-metal groans of the van's engine seemed louder since leaving the freeway. We were climbing the hill to Miss's house when it happened. The van rumbled—a low, painful sound—as it gradually slowed.

Miss frowned. "I've got the pedal all the way down."

I glanced back at Mamá. She sat up, her eyes darting. They landed on me. A warm smile made cracks across her broken lips.

I had to smile back.

At a stop sign, Miss braked. When she stepped on the gas, instead of lurching forward, the van rolled back.

"Whoa!" Miss turned the wheel, and the van slid downhill, neatly parked against the curb. She yanked on the emergency brake. "The transmission."

"But you can fix it, Miss?"

She shook her head. "A new one would cost more than the whole thing is worth."

Miss reached into her purse and pulled out Ethan's phone. She glanced at it, then dropped it back in her purse, irritated.

Then she said a word she never planned to teach me. But I already knew what it meant.

I didn't mind walking up the hill to Miss's house. Fruit trees had blossomed, making the air sweet. Birds called to one another, squirrels and rabbits darted from yard to yard, as if Snow White's woodland friends had moved into the *barrio blanco* with her.

Ethan ran ahead, anxious to get home.

Holding Mamá's warm, rough hand on one side and Miss's cool, smooth hand on the other, I walked up the hill.

My pinkie looped around Miss's index finger. Mamá and I kept giving each other loving little squeezes. We didn't hurry.

But it was over too quickly.

When the Dahl house came into view, Mamá gasped. I tried to see what she saw. *A mansion? A magical castle?* To me, it was simply a house. A home where a family lived and ate and fought and laughed.

Then I remembered Miss hadn't only lost her job. She and her boys were going to lose their home—just like my family. But we'd figured it out. And so would they.

The garage doors stood open, like the house wore a lopsided grin. Rosa ran out squealing. She threw herself into our mother's arms. Watching them was like having my insides sucked out. I wanted to be part of their happiness, but too many other feelings sloshed around inside me. Then Rosa pulled me into a tight circle with Mamá. "Papi called! He is working in Tijuana to make money to pay a coyote."

"*¡Gracias a Dios!*" said Mamá—thank God!

Then it hit me. *Gracias. Grace.*

Rosa burst into tears, hugging me. "Thank you for bringing Mamá home safe."

I hugged her back, but it felt like someone else was inside me, making my arms and legs move. I hadn't brought Mamá home safe. Because life isn't safe.

And life is never fair. It still felt like life *should* be fair. But now I know better. We can only go forward with hope while we pray for *grace.*

It's the best we can do.

When I let go of Rosa, I noticed the scar across her eyebrow where the hair refused to grow back. The slant of it made her look angry. The image of Victor's scarred eyelid flashed in my mind.

I reached up with one careful finger. "Did I—?"

"*Está bien,*" she said, pulling away.

The scar ruined Rosa's perfect face. As long as we lived, that ugly mark would tell everyone about the very worst in me. About my meanness. I felt small. Like I was shrinking inside myself. "What do your friends say?"

She shrugged. "I tell them I walked into a door."

She lies? To hide my badness? A moment before, I'd thought I couldn't feel any worse. I whispered, "Can you forgive me?"

Rosa surprised me with a wide grin. "You're my *sister!*"

I looked away so I wouldn't cry.

Faces swirled around me. Like being inside a 3-D movie. But I should've been sitting in the audience with a box of popcorn, because I didn't feel like part of what was happening on the screen.

I looked around again and was surprised to see Cody standing next to me.

"Hi," he said.

After the trauma and drama—the long drive and sleepless hours, the descent into cavernous depths, a daring rescue and a tearful reunion—Cody squinted at me and said, "Hi."

The word for that is *anticlimactic*.

I looked past his glasses, past the ghostly reflections of myself, straight into his eyes. He was as tall as me — as tall as *I*. I grabbed his arm. "I need to ask you something."

He stepped back, his eyes wide. *"What?"*

"What's your favorite ballet?"

His shoulders relaxed. *"Dracula.* It's great. Lots of blood."

I nodded. It did sound great.

"I want to show you something." He led me to the porch and pulled a rusty pair of clippers from the box of gardening tools. With quick snips he cut several flower stalks with many bell-shaped blossoms and handed them to me.

Pink and purple. Hope and sorrow. They looked like the flowers I'd painted on my picture frame. The day I'd met Miss.

Even nicer than the soft spring colors was the fragrance.

"Hyacinth," he said.

The first time I'd been to the Dahl house, I'd

been too late to see the hyacinths. They were ugly, I'd thought. I hadn't *appreciated* them.

But it hadn't been their time to bloom.

My eyes started to water.

"Yeah," said Cody. "They do that to me, too. I can't stop sneezing."

MISS didn't make a speech before we drove away, telling Rosa and me to have a good life, study hard, and get scholarships. She just gave us each a quick hug. She even gave Mamá a hug.

Mamá leaned against me in the taxi, and pretty soon she was nodding. The jar of hyacinths was in my lap. Cody said he wanted me to have them so I'd recognize them when I saw them again. I couldn't guess how long that'd be.

I thought Rosa might start asking me about our trip, but I didn't think I could scrape together the words to explain. My emotions rolled around inside me like waves.

As though she heard me thinking, my sister reached over and took my hand. My pinkie wrapped around her index finger. A sad smile touched her lips.

She whispered in English, "It is better this way. Mamá needs us now."

Rosa is right. We need to put Mamá first. To be there for her, until she's strong enough to be there for herself.

It's what families do. And it's not because we *have* to. It's what we *choose* to do.

But choices come with a price. I looked into Rosa's eyes and let her see my soul.

She said softly, "You do not have to give up everything. You can take French in high school. The bus goes by the recreation center. You can show Suelita gymnastics, and I can teach her to swim."

"We should start reading to her," I whispered back.

"I will read in Spanish, and you read to her in English."

"You need to teach *me* to read and write in Spanish," I said.

Rosa smiled. "No way! I cannot let you get ahead of me!"

But I know she'll teach me. She has to. I'm going to write French and Spanish translations for Hollywood movies.

And someday I'll write my own screenplay.

Maybe Ethan will direct it.

By the time we crossed *la línea*—the line between the white neighborhood and our barrio—I felt better.

I will find the missing pieces of Mamá—even if only in the mirror.

If Papi doesn't come back, I will use my power to rescue him, too.

And though I still want Miss, I no longer need her. I will be the one to make things happen in my life. I can do it better than Miss, because I have one foot in my Mexican heritage and one foot in the country where I was born and educated. That is something Miss can never have. I can walk *la línea*—the line between her world and that of my people.

I will be part of both.

A phone rang. Mamá sat up and looked around.

Reaching into her pocket, Rosa smiled an apology to me. "Miss got it for me. In case she needed to reach me."

The claw of the beast, now scarcely more than a pinprick, nicked my heart. Rosa answered the phone, and I heard the tinny version of Miss's musical voice. I couldn't hear her words, but it was a question.

"Hang on. I'll ask." Rosa gave me a wide grin. "The youth center has tickets for the ballet. *Romeo and Juliet.* You want to go?"

The sting in my heart ebbed away. My smile slipped sideways. A smirk. "Could I talk to Miss?"

Rosa passed me the phone.

For once, I took a moment to *think* before opening my mouth. Then in my own musical voice I spoke. *"Oui, madame! Bien sûr! J'adore le ballet! Merci beaucoup!"*

Rosa giggled, and Mamá smiled.

Through the phone I heard a snort.

Just as it takes a village to raise a child, it takes a metropolis to write a book. I need to recognize my first and best teachers, the authors of every book I have ever read, those who continue to reach out to me, bridging time and space, infecting me with their magic. They've taught me how to write, and more — they've made it plain why we must write. Most important, they've made me *want* to write.

Many thanks to the Society of Children's Book Writers and Illustrators, Rocky Mountain Fiction Writers, and Pikes Peak Writers for their exceptional conferences. A special shout-out to the literary agents, editors, authors, and other presenters who attend these events and are so generous with their knowledge.

I would not have made it to this point without my dear friends at Boulder Writers' Workshop and my writing coach, Lori DeBoer. All my love to my critique groups, the Arapahoe Library District, and especially my own mentors, Kathryn Jens and Linda Baggus, who were with Jacinta from the start.

Warm appreciation to the community in northeast Littleton, the inspiration for the fictional town of Maplewood, including the City of Littleton, South Suburban Parks and Recreation, Littleton Public Schools, GracePoint Community Church, North Littleton Promise, Littleton Immigrant Integration Initiative, Save Our Youth, and Whiz Kids.

I am indebted to my talented agent, Sean McCarthy; the Sheldon Fogelman Agency; my gifted editor, Andrea Tompa; and Candlewick Press for faith in me and my work. A bouquet of colors to Sara Palacios for the stunning jacket art.

My gratitude flows to my husband, Larry, for putting up with me; my cousin Bruce Robbins, official photographer and unofficial "dad" to four giggly teenagers on the research trip to Carlsbad Caverns; my best friend and first editor, Vickie Robb; and the many others who've read and provided feedback on this novel—especially those who read it multiple times. I am particularly grateful to the readers who took the time to give me advice and insight on issues of cultural accuracy. Any issues that remain are my own.

This work is a testament to my mom, Carol Robbins, who always told me I could do anything I wanted to do.

Look Both Ways in the Barrio Blanco is lovingly dedicated to Rubi and Perla for trusting a pushy white lady with their secrets and for continuing to allow me to "kidnap" them after that first scary time; their little sister, Esmé, who has stopped slapping me and now likes going out with Miss; their lovely mother, for her strength and gracious ways; and Forrest and August, now tall, handsome young men, who continue to come along for the ride.